THE MISFORTUNES OF NIGEL

Fiona
Pitt-Kethley

THE M*I*SFORTUNES
OF N*I*GEL

PETER OWEN

LONDON AND CHESTER SPRINGS PA

U.S. DISTRIBUTOR
DUFOUR EDITIONS
CHESTER SPRINGS,
PA 19425-0449
(215) 458-5005

PETER OWEN PUBLISHERS
73 Kenv ay Road London SW5 0RE
Peter Owen books are distributed in the USA by
Dufour Editions Inc. Chester Springs PA 19425–0449

First published in Great Britain 1991
© Fiona Pitt-Kethley 1991

British Library Cataloguing in Publication Data
Pitt-Kethley, Fiona *1954–*
The misfortunes of Nigel.
I. Title
823.914 [F]

ISBN 0–7206–0830–9

Printed in Great Britain by Billings of Worcester

The Misfortunes of Nigel is a work of fiction
and the characters therein are not
intended to resemble any persons living
or dead.

THE MISFORTUNES OF NIGEL

CHAPTER

1

'IT IS A UNIVERSAL BUT UNACKNOWLEDGED TRUTH THAT A MAN who thinks women are rotten will end up with a rotten woman,' Aunty Mildred warned her youngest nephew one Christmas.

Nigel had been playing chess with his father and had just lost his queen. 'Doesn't matter,' he'd said. 'She's only a bloody woman. Plenty more where she came from. I'll make all my pawns into queens.' Two moves later it was checkmate. He cried and his nanny put him to bed. Then he called for his mother to tell him a story.

She sat by him, in silk and pearls, smelling of perfume, and began: 'Once upon a time, there was a boy called Nigel Charles Hughes. He came from a rich family and was very good-looking. He had a remarkable power over women. They all fancied him and thought he was the handsomest boy they had ever seen.' She leant across and kissed him good night. He fell asleep with a smile on his face. That was all he remembered clearly from those days. He sometimes wondered later how his mother would have gone on with the story.

Years afterwards, while at a minor public school, Nigel was frequently heard to say to those he fagged for, 'Women are just slags. They don't know how to behave. They have it easy. They just rip off men and live off them.' He couldn't quite tell where he had got it from − the papers or his relatives (they were not all old curmudgeons like Mildred) − but it sounded sophisticated and true.

At the age of nineteen, Nigel met the woman who was to be his wife. Gina came from a circus family. She had been born in Naples, where the family often spent their summers.

Nigel lay back on the grass at the edge of a car park in Santa Lucia and watched her family perform. It was a warm, early July evening. He had landed at Naples that morning, coming from Palermo. He was travelling alone and had got talking to Gina's father in a café on the docks. The man spoke a mixture of French and English. He sold him a ticket for the night's performance, talking of the beauty of his daughter who would be in the show, and also told him of a hotel owned by a friend where he could stay cheaply.

Nigel was looking up Gina's tutu, not really watching the performance. He took the bottom of her lacy leotard to be her knickers. She had not been in the earlier acts. He was glad of that. An older woman had been encircled with knives on a revolving target. The father, whose name was Serge, had talked of the circus being mainly a family act. Two brothers had balanced, clowning on low wires to music from a wind-up gramophone playing on top of one of the cars. For their next trick they juggled the father's set of knives, demonstrating their sharpness first by slicing cleanly through a head of fennel. Nigel thought he saw scars on the wrist of one of the brothers, but maybe it was a trick of the light. Then the fakir was announced and a more oriental record put on. El Khalil was not one of the family, Nigel had learnt from Serge that morning. He did things like sticking hat pins in his cheek, stubbing out the audience's cigarettes on his bald head, and blowing fire. The night Nigel was there, he just ate fire, then lay down on the road, balancing a board full of nails on his chest. Gina came and stepped up on top, given a helping hand by her father. Nigel was impressed immediately by her imperious, dominating expression. She was striking in an unusual sort of way. Her light brown hair was piled up and threaded with cheap necklaces culminating in an ostrich feather. She had been announced as 'Principessa Gina'. She had heavy gold make-up round her eyes. Her skin was an olive colour only a shade lighter than her hair. When he lay back and closed one eye, he could see

10

her strange, exaggerated, proud profile with its thin Roman nose silhouetted against the sea. Then there were the lacy knickers....

At the end of the show, Gina brought round a soft floppy hat belonging to one of her clowning brothers. She had a younger girl behind her in a miniskirt. Nigel believed he was the only person in the audience with a proper ticket; it had a number on it like a raffle ticket. The other spectators put some small change in the hat. They were just passers-by who had stopped to see the show. Gina waited in front of him for money. He showed his ticket but she looked mystified, so he dug out some change of his own and asked her in English if she would like to have a pizza with him. She looked vague again, so he put his request into faltering Italian. He had been travelling round Italy for the last two weeks and had picked up a few phrases.

Gina understood at once and took him to a nearby restaurant where they had their pizzas and a lot of rough *Gragnano* wine. Afterwards they went back to his hotel. It was Nigel's first experience. His parents had put a stop to most of the relationships, usually with girls from shops, that he had tried to form at home. Nigel had had so much wine that he could not remember much in the morning. Gina was sobbing then. He couldn't understand everything she was saying but she seemed to resent the night before. The proprietor asked for her identity papers and charged extra for the room. Nigel would be paying the full price for his double from now on. At twelve o'clock Gina left saying she would return. She got the proprietor to interpret.

Gina came back at night with a few clothes – all her things, she said. He hung her tights and tutus and the one proper dress she owned next to his own shirts in the wardrobe. He fantasized about being married and having women's clothes mixed with his permanently.

Nigel spent the next few weeks with Gina. He even offered to help in the show. He wondered if he had hidden talents her father could bring out. Would he be able to walk on the wire or clown a bit? He drew the line at messing with fire or knives. At the end of August it was time for the family to move on. Suddenly, Gina said she was pregnant and Nigel was made to do the right thing. It had to be his, the family argued, because Gina was a virgin when she met him. Surely he'd noticed? She had plenty of admirers — soldiers, the fakir, most of the men in the audiences — but she had been brought up a good Catholic like her mother before her and had not done a thing with them. She had only let Nigel take her to his hotel because she loved him.

It was more of a knife than a shotgun marriage. It was celebrated in Britain. Serge alone came across with Gina, leaving his family in France where they would be performing for the next few weeks. Nigel's parents were furious at first. They had cherished hopes of a society match for their good-looking youngest son. They had sent him to Europe, telling friends it was for his education, but telling him it was to prise him away from the slags back home; now they were punished for their snobbishness. He'd come back with someone they definitely didn't approve of and who didn't speak a word of English.

When Nigel's and Gina's son arrived, Nigel was left holding the baby. He had slight doubts about whether it was his, fair as it was. Sometimes he sensed his grandfather's stern jaw, at other times he saw only the dark brooding eyes of the mock-fakir, El Khalil.

Nigel had thought he was clever to cut out the competition. He always felt a need to prove he could get the girl from other men in any situation. There were bitter moments, though, when he believed that Gina would have been anyone's against a wall for a meal or a bottle of plonk or other minor material assets. Had Gina spotted him for someone rich and gullible, he wondered? He'd boasted about the wealth of his parents in horrible phrasebook Italian.

CHAPTER
2

AFTER HIS MARRIAGE NIGEL MANAGED ON MONEY FROM HIS PARENTS. His father kept lecturing him, telling him to be a man and get a proper job. Within a few months he cut off his allowance as the only way to make him do anything. Nigel had been good at English at school so he naturally fell into writing. He had enough contacts from his schooldays to make it easy to get some work published without touting it round the way an outsider would have had to. He also got a job lecturing at a sixth-form college one day a week. He began to make enough for his family to survive on. That wasn't enough for Gina, though.

Sometimes Nigel would come back from delivering an article and find his son deserted and screaming in wet nappies. On those occasions, Gina would be gone for days and he'd be left not knowing what to do. She wasn't kind or even sexy any more but he missed her presence all the same. He was frightened of being left alone at night.

His parents had been glittering socialites in their younger days. They loved him but hadn't spent enough time with him to convince him of this. Still, they were responsible people. They would never have left him alone. They didn't need to — they could afford a nanny. In fact they'd had a succession of them. One of the nannies had had a soldier boyfriend and used to leave young Nigel for hours while she went to dances, threatening him with various supernatural horrors if he told on her. These days he laughed at such things, but sometimes in the still of the night he'd wake up in a cold sweat remembering the old terrors.

He tackled Gina feebly when she came back. She had picked up a little English now, so communication was getting easier. She would never tell him exactly where she'd been, though. She had been bored. He was a very boring husband. That was all she would say. Usually she was sporting some new clothes — nothing all that pricey, but perhaps too much to have come out of the housekeeping.

After a while he stopped asking. If he had been left alone and needed to go out, he would just take the kid round to his parents'. It was crawling now. Gina had to go and give Italian lessons, he would say in explanation. His parents began to have some slight respect for her. It sounded as if she was chipping in and trying to pull her weight in another country. Perhaps she had not been such a bad match for their son, after all.

Nigel began to watch Gina and tried to check up on her. It wasn't easy. Most of her disappearances coincided with one of his own trips out. He began to go out less and less. He gave up his one-day-a-week teaching job and stayed inside, his hair getting long and lank. He took a few chops at it himself but it didn't make it look any better. He started to get dirty. There was a certain logic to this. The less he shaved and washed, the less times per year he would have to go out and get soap. He posted his articles in the postbox at the end of the road, which was within sight of his front door, instead of taking them into editors' offices. Often they arrived late, and he lost jobs because of this. He turned his cheques over to Gina to bank for him. Sometimes she did and sometimes she didn't. Sometimes she would say she had lost them and he would ring up the editor concerned only to find that the cheque had been cashed. She needed money, of course, for their food and so on, but he wished she had told him. At times he felt she was creaming a little off regularly and setting it aside somewhere as a fund for something. If she was, he didn't want to know. She was his wife and the wife of a clever chap like him must be above suspicion. He couldn't have got it *that* wrong.

One day Nigel was invited to lunch with an old school friend who worked for a newspaper. It would lead to a better, more regular job, he hoped. Gina was invited as well. She spent hours dressing. The time was getting later and later. They could still make it by taxi, he thought. Five minutes before they had to leave, she decided not to go. 'Your friends will not like me,' she said and burst into tears. He went alone. When he came back she was gone. He went to pick up his son Anthony from his parents'. This time he was frank with them.

'You must get a divorce,' they said. 'Old McCall will do the job — bit expensive, but thorough. You can come and live here for a while until things are sorted out.'

The next morning he was sorry he had told them. Divorce? He'd look a fool to his friends. He never got things wrong. He was clever pulling an exotic wife — someone that other men had wanted. Besides, she might claim part of the house that he was paying for and that his parents had put the deposit on. He went back home. If anyone was to leave anyone it should be he. He packed his things, then remembered she'd never notice if he went. He would have to wait till she came back and then leave. That would serve her right.

Nigel came and went more freely in the lonely months that followed. A few days after Gina had gone he picked up a piece of paper that was blowing around on the platform at Archway, his nearest tube station. It was a receipt for a train ticket to Naples. Was it Gina's? Probably not. Thousands of people used even that small station and thousands of people went to Naples, though not usually by train.

He searched her things and found nothing personal. She had left most of her clothes. They were only ones from jumble sales, anyway. A mountain of old shoes, some damp and mildewy, cascaded out of the bottom of the wardrobe and a grubby pair of knickers hung on the knob of their chest of drawers. He buried his nose in these but decided that they only smelt of nylon and threw them away. The shoes he kicked back into the cupboard, pulling a box across the doors to hold them in.

He decided not to have anything around that reminded him of her. Even their wedding photo was put away. Then he turned and saw the kid. It said 'Mamma!' and cried and looked as horribly like her as a little boy could. He did not feel very fatherly. He longed to leave his son with his parents permanently and would have done so if only he could have been sure they wouldn't say 'I told you so!'

When anyone asked, Nigel told them that his wife was staying with her parents — one of them was ill. Indeed, that might have been the truth for all he knew. He had tried ringing them. They were not on the phone, of course, but if they were spending this summer in Naples, then Serge was probably parked in that little bar in the docks during the day. Nigel had a beer mat from there, which gave the address and number. He'd kept it as a sort of sentimental trophy of his first meeting with Gina's family. When he rang, the proprietor asked how Gina was, then went off to look for her father, leaving the phone off the hook. Minutes later Nigel put it down fearing the phone bill. He didn't bother to write. He knew her parents weren't keen on putting pen to paper. He had done all any husband could be expected to do.

CHAPTER
3

FOUR MONTHS AFTER GINA HAD GONE, NIGEL WOKE UP WITH A START to find the baby crying in the cot beside his bed and a stranger in his room.

'What are you doing?' he quavered. He could just make out the man against the light. He was short and exotic-looking – Malaysian, perhaps, with large earrings and an upside-down crucifix hanging round his neck.

'I'm looking for the other couple who live here,' the man said with perfect confidence. 'Gina.... You know Gina?'

'Of course I know Gina,' Nigel said stiffly. 'She's my wife. Well, she's not here at the moment. She's with her parents. One of them's sick, you know.'

'Ah, so you must be the husband,' the man said. 'I know a lot about you.' He laughed, a little contemptuously, Nigel thought, but maybe it was his imagination.

'What are you doing in here?'

'I have the key Gina gave me. She said I could come any time. Didn't you know?' He laughed again.

'I think you must have misunderstood and I don't know how you got hold of that. Here, give me the key.'

'But of course . . . if you think that's wise. Gina will be very angry.'

The man left and Nigel put away the spare key. Who did he think he was, the little foreign whippersnapper? He could deal with that sort and he could deal with his wife when she came back. She would come back, of course. Women couldn't manage on their own. They weren't clever enough.

Gina did come back a week later and she *was* very angry. She asked him for money the minute she came in. 'I had to go away,' she said, 'because you are so boring.' When she heard that her friend had been asked to leave, she was even more angry. She hit Nigel about the head repeatedly with the phone book, knocking off the glasses he wore for reading when he was on his own. 'Alain is my business manager,' she said. 'Nigel, you should have asked him to stay and made up a spare bed for him.'

'Your business manager?' Nigel said. 'You don't have a business!'

'I am an artiste!' she said and stamped out of the room.

After that there was a succession of odd artistes and agents coming to the house. Sometimes they were Gina's agents, sometimes she was theirs. She kept telling him that they produced real art, not like his writing. One day Nigel came in to find a man standing in the living room with his flies undone and a silly smile on his face.

'He is doing his act!' Gina said before Nigel had time to ask. 'He is practising it for the Edinburgh Festival – the Fringe. Show him, Phil.'

Phil pulled some razor blades out of his pocket and proceeded to eat them. His other hand was pointing his cock around as he hopped on one leg.

'Oh, he is so funny!' Gina laughed. Nigel did not laugh. He was reassured, though, to find it was all an act, even if the man wasn't very good. He noticed he had cut his lower lip on the razor blades. 'Modern blades aren't as crunchable as the old variety,' Phil said in explanation as the blood dripped off his chin on to the carpet.

The acts who came to their house got on Nigel's nerves. He spent more and more time away. He taught courses in journalism at obscure creative-writing schools all over the country. He missed trains back, accidentally on purpose, and stayed away as long as he could. After a short writer-in-residence position lasting three weeks at a library in Manchester, he came back to what he had hoped for – no Gina. Most of her things had gone and the house was in a filthy mess. He rang his parents and found that she had left Anthony there a week ago. They thought he knew all about it. 'I'm coming home!' he said. He spent that evening clearing up and went to the estate agent's in the morning to put his house on the market. He fervently hoped that she would stay away a long time, then come back to nothing.

The house was sold quickly as he did not care about getting the full price. He moved into his parents' house in Chelsea. They were not thrilled about having him and the child back, but felt they had to help – anything to get him away from his dreadful Gina.

There was room enough, anyway. It was one of those rambling millionaire residences in Old Church Street. It had a conservatory and a large garden. Little Anthony loved running about in it and, as he got older, he used to climb over into the garden next door. The house there had been empty a long time. There was some silly tale about a nasty feeling, a kind of presence there, that had made it hard to sell or let. It had been on the agent's books for years. Two pop-star couples had owned it for a while, and then a writer, but things had happened to them or their families: serious depression, drug addiction. Nigel didn't believe in hauntings and never warned Anthony about the old house. If he wanted to play there, fine. He himself had played in other people's houses as a boy. He had liked to break into the homes of plebs – not to steal, just to see how the other half lived. It was obviously a natural part of any boy's growing-up. He had decided to send Anthony to a state school. His current editor had socialist leanings and Nigel got on well with him. He was given more work by flogging how poor he was, bringing up a son alone, and so on. He still used the old Archway address for his cheques if he did not collect them. The new owners were quite amenable to forwarding his mail. They had a naive enjoyment of doing something for a young writer.

Nigel was beginning to feel more content with his new life style. He was much better off now, living at his parents' house and having everything taken care of. These days his sheets were laundered for him – there was no Gina to send him to the Launderette. He often dined out. His father usually paid. The only thing missing in his life was sex.

He toyed with the idea of divorce, but he didn't want the public acknowledgement of failure. So he decided to get a mistress. However, mistresses can be hard to come by. Women seemed to want to know a lot about him and asked why his wife had left. He thought they were very impertinent.

Nigel was good-looking, with that refinement of skin that comes from generations of money. There had been no difficulties in his upbringing, nothing to spoil his hands or wear him out. By his late twenties he still looked nineteen. He had the beginnings of a kind of uneasy, Dorian Gray over-youngness. In later years people would come to joke that he must have a disgusting, wrinkly portrait hanging in the attic. On looks alone, Nigel would have found it pretty easy to pull almost any one of a number of attractive women. He dressed fashionably. When he asked anyone out they were usually thrilled. He wondered, though, why nothing seemed to last. Behind his back, female colleagues sometimes complained about the crass remarks he let slip about women.

'We don't review books by women in our paper,' he told them, 'because there simply aren't any good ones to write about.' He said it and he meant it. He was firmly convinced that nothing a woman did came up to what he and his male friends were capable of. Nasty, psychoanalysing females told him that with this attitude there was no possibility of his forming a lasting relationship. It was true that he was frequently dropped, but he knew the real reason for that. 'Pretty little thing,' he would say to his male friends, 'but she wasn't woman enough to hold me.'

His parents tried to make matches for him. He resented their attempts on principle and generated his own series of pick-ups. He could have done without sex happily enough if only modern culture hadn't convinced him that it was part of man's lot. Gina had never been kind about his sexual performance and she was the only woman he'd had. He had bragged about having a lot more − men have to keep their ends up with each other − but in fact he had not got as far with the other women in his life. Some had tried to seduce him. On being refused, the more vindictive ones had hinted that Gina was right to accuse him of sexual inadequacy. (He had often been too frank about her remarks to him in an attempt to gain sympathy.) One cruder woman told him he was a miser — someone too mean to give a drop of anything away.

In the first years of his marriage, Nigel found he could only have sex with Gina after she had fought him. She often laid into him physically, gave him bruises and black eyes, stamped on his feet and broke his toes, ripped up his books, the lot. He knew men didn't hit back so he would just hold her off and dodge the blows, or cover his head with a pillow. Afterwards, if she had not stormed out, he would fuck her to punish her. He knew nice women didn't enjoy such things. Gina often said that she didn't. She would lie back and think of Italy, or the circus fakir, or Alain or Phil or any of the others. If he failed to come so much better. When he did that, she would say, 'You have not performed your marital rights, but thank you for trying.' He liked the phrase 'marital rights'. It wasn't common like 'fucking'. His mother had once talked about fucking and it had put him right off her.

Nigel's pick-ups were usually what he defined as 'shop-girls'. He could manage the slick chat-up easier with them than with fellow professionals. He kept a good knowledge of the Top Twenty because he knew that was what they would like to talk about. He enjoyed going into travel agents' and boasting about the holidays his parents had paid for, or else having his thick, silky mass of dark blond hair cut in a unisex salon. He liked service from women. Sometimes he asked the girls out, sometimes not. He usually managed to pick up odd names he could use in conversations with other men. In fact, hairdressers were the most useful ones. 'Went out with Tracy last night — only just sixteen, blond hair, what a raver — gave me a blow job the first time we met.' He used that gag time and time again, just changing the name or the age (by a few months) to show he didn't get stuck with anybody or taken in. It was a great act. He was good-looking enough for it to sound possible. 'Lucky old Nigel!' all the men said. By thirty he had all the spiel of a dirty old man.

On the odd occasions when he did go out with someone, he would talk passionately, hint at a holiday in the sun with them, then say that unfortunately he had a later engagement that night, or a review to finish by the morning. Otherwise they would have gone on to great things. He would then give them his number. If they rang that showed his mother he could find someone on his own without any help from her. He used to fix a date with a new girlfriend, then cancel it at the last minute. That got rid of most of them without complications. Any more persistent ones could be got rid of by the odd cutting remark. Nigel's journalistic work had given him quite a talent for that sort of thing.

CHAPTER
4

'HEY, NIGEL, MUMMY'S BACK!' ANTHONY SAID. IT WAS MUMMY, NOT Mamma now. At nine, Anthony had lost most of his baby Italian.

'Stop your bloody lies! Haven't I told you we won't be seeing her again?' Nigel was deep in an article that had to be delivered that afternoon. He always left things as late as possible.

'No, honestly, Dad! She's living next door.'

Nigel wrote it off as little boys' lies. He hoped he would not have to send Anthony to a psychologist. He didn't want any nonsense about imaginary companions. Perhaps I should buy him a dog? he thought.

When he came back from delivering his article, his mother called to him. 'You won't believe what's happened,' she said. 'Your wife's back, cool as a cucumber — the cheek of it! Worse still, she's living next door — squatting.'

That was only the start of it. While Gina would no longer live with Nigel, neither would she get out of his life completely. She wouldn't mind her own child or do anything useful. Occasionally, she took him from the garden and disappeared for hours. Anthony would usually come back sick and hyperactive, having been fed pounds of highly coloured sweets. 'Mummy stole them from Woolworths,' he said.

If it wasn't sweets it was unsuitable playthings like knives. 'You must put your foot down!' Nigel's father said, the day Anthony came back with blood pouring from his hand. They had rushed him to the Royal Marsden for stitches. There wasn't any serious damage, but he would have a thin, white scar up his middle finger for life. Anthony was to become absurdly self-conscious about this minor defect in later years and usually hid his left hand in his pocket or under his desk.

Gina had of course been trying to initiate Anthony into the family trade of knife-throwing. She had offered him a full set of throwing knives for Christmas. She had tried to rope in the little girl from the house opposite to be blindfolded and stood up against the old apple tree at the bottom of the garden. 'We will play at William Tell,' she'd said. 'It's better with a knife than an arrow.'

The little girl was no fool, though. She ran home crying, 'The foreign lady opposite wanted to throw knives at me!' and was smacked for telling lies.

By autumn, Gina's family had all moved in – apparently to stay. They had worked in the circus for generations. They were an amalgam of nationalities. Gina's paternal grandmother had been Russian. She had come over to join the rest of the family in Italy without speaking a word of Italian. Tragically, the local authorities had popped her into an asylum assuming her homesick mutterings and failure to communicate were due to other reasons. She had died there soon afterwards. Gina's grandfather was French. He had brought the surname Buffon into the family. He was a fire-eater as well as a knife-thrower. Now solo, he still practised these skills as a busker in squares throughout Europe. The circus was a small family operation; they rarely used animals, although they had a half-starved pet monkey for a while. Mostly they concentrated on things that could be set up easily at fairgrounds, such as low-wire walking, clowning and juggling. When they could, they had married people with other skills. Gina's brother Herve had hooked a goldfish-eater. He was practising fire-eating, too. They both performed in the kitchen. It was large and airy and Herve could always get a light from the stove. The whole family deeply despised Nigel because he could not do anything useful. They had got him to pass the hat round for them once or twice when he first met Gina in Italy, but in their opinion he wasn't even good at that – he always gave the right change.

The family's performances centred round a kind of sado-masochism, playing on the cruelty and fear of the audience. None of their acts were skilled in the finest sense. They concentrated on things that kept the audience on the edge of their seats waiting for death or disfigurement. They were scorched by flames, grazed by knives, and fell off wires regularly. It was what their audiences liked. Nigel desperately wanted to keep Anthony from that sort of life. Anthony was sensitive, he thought, just like he was. He put a timid ban on the knives.

In one of his rare conversations with Gina he asked how on earth they would all earn a living in London. 'My brothers all do acts in clubs,' she said. 'My sister will, I think, too. Father is leaving his knife-throwing. He has a good job with a London council.'

Curiously, it was possible that Serge could become a council employee. Although he was in reality French-Russian and had for years spent the greater part of his summers in Italy, he was technically a British citizen. By a stroke of luck or something, he had been born under canvas while his family were performing in Malta. The job, it turned out, was that of grave-digger. Serge had a strong, thuggish build which would come in useful there, Nigel thought snobbishly.

Serge looked so thuggish, in fact, that he was able to intimidate almost anybody. Nigel's mother had been a ballerina in her youth. She had no desire or need to give dancing lessons now, but she was forced into it by Serge on behalf of his younger daughter, Yvette. Yvette was what Nigel termed a 'bad-rubber kid'. These late, unwanted children always resent their position and cause the maximum mayhem and trouble. Yvette came on like a nymphomaniac and then showed all the shock of a raped nun at any response. She was fifteen. Her loving father wanted her to be a Page-Three model and make all their fortunes. The only problem was she had no tits. She pretended to be eighteen and got herself a job as a go-go dancer in a Soho club. That was why Serge thought she needed ballet lessons.

Nigel's mother tolerated her partly for fear of the father and partly out of pity for an unwanted, awkward child. She tolerated her, that is, until she made a pass at William, Nigel's older brother. While his wife was in the garden, Yvette came in, got on William's lap, put her hand on his balls, told him he was more of a man than his brother and then suggested he set her up in a flat as his mistress. He said he wasn't tempted, not being the fool that his brother was. Nigel resented that remark for years. William's own wife was a highly articulate, hard-working businesswoman, thoroughly approved of by her in-laws. After climbing on William's lap, Yvette tried to claim rape and there was a frightful scene all over the road at 3 a.m. The next morning, Nigel's father called them all in for a discussion. He was tight-lipped and white with rage. That was the only time Nigel had ever seen him angry.

'My son William wouldn't touch you or your family with a barge pole,' he said. 'Marrying Gina was the biggest mistake that Nigel ever made and he's paid for it ever since. Personally I wish he'd end it tomorrow. All right, go to the police as you threaten. You certainly won't get any money out of me for this. Remember one thing – this trumped-up case will be tried in an English court of law. Whose word do you think the judge is going to believe – that of a wealthy respectable businessman, who went to the same public school and university probably as himself, or that of an under-age tramp who got herself an unsavoury job on false pretences, who lives in a squat and doesn't speak very good English? I should think you'll either find yourselves deported or popped into gaol for wasting police time.'

They saw the point and went home. There were no more dancing lessons after that. Perhaps Yvette had learnt all she needed to know.

For several weeks things were quiet. At Christmas the bluster of Gina's father was succeeded by the wheedling manner of her mother. 'I bet she's a shoplifter or a pickpocket with that sneaky look,' Mrs Hughes said.

Mme Buffon was always borrowing this and that, and never returned anything – cup and sugar would disappear together, packets of coffee, loaves of bread. In the end Mrs Hughes ordered the cook to say that they did not have whatever she asked for. Being Spanish, the cook repeated these instructions word for word and a lot of offence was taken.

Still, polite as she usually was, Mrs Hughes was extremely glad when relations were at last broken off. She dreaded that her son would be foolish enough to patch up the marriage and take off with Gina again. She also dreaded that Yvette would get one of her other sons into trouble. She wanted no further connection with the family.

Even though there were no more invasions, the Hugheses were still conscious of the Buffon family next door. There were ghastly screaming quarrels in the middle of the night, to which the police were often called. Gina hardly sounded human when she was in the middle of one of these, and would bark incoherently. 'You don't think we ought to call the RSPCA?' Nigel's father said sarcastically. 'Somebody's torturing a Jack Russell in there.' Nigel knew only too well whose voice it was. He'd had to share a house with it for years.

Without seeing her, Nigel was always reminded of Gina. He liked to flatter himself that she made her presence felt out of passion for him. Gina had bought herself a guitar recently. Presumably she felt singing might be a safer career than knife-throwing.

Her first attempts were on a country-and-western song. It had just three chords in it. The only bit Nigel could hear floating over the wall was, 'It's the cowboys' Christmas party tonight. . . . Uh, huh!' He didn't like to knock the wife he had chosen publicly, but even he had to admit over dinner with friends that the singer next door was unlikely to make it in a big way.

He began listening out for the wails as he sat at his typewriter every morning. The song even haunted him in his sleep. He began to feel like sending her some new lyrics anonymously, but changed his mind once he found out the price of sheet music.

Eventually there was silence. He was able to get on with his book reviews in peace. Day after day of blessed silence. After six weeks, unobservant as he was, he realized why. The house next door was empty again. Gina and family had gone.

That night he tackled his mother. She must have written to the owner to get them evicted. She denied all knowledge: 'I expect somebody else in the road did it,' she said. 'That sort of family brings down the price of property.'

Nigel asked around. If they were going to go, he would have liked to have had something to do with the eviction. He should have been the one to send in the bailiffs. He didn't like being left in ignorance of what had happened. The little girl opposite was the only person who seemed to know a thing. 'Oh, they went when I was going to school for my swimming competition,' she said. 'They put all their things in a big van with "Buffoon's Cabaret" on the side. Daddy said a buffoon is a fool and cabaret is . . .'

'I know what a cabaret is,' Nigel cut in. He didn't like smart-arse little girls.

CHAPTER
5

HIS LIFE STABILIZED FOR A WHILE. GINA WAS GONE. ANTHONY WAS now away at school. He could get on with his grander literary aims. He would write novels. It wasn't difficult for Nigel to get a good contract from a big publishing house. He had a name in journalism and, more importantly, he had a lot of contacts, old school friends and so on, in publishing. He fancied doing a cynical novel of London life. There would be a lot of London clubs in it and a hero who screwed his way through a succession of beautiful women. Nigel already had himself cast as the hero. He would have to get out a lot more to do the research.

In fact, for the next few months, all he did was research. He had a year to write the book and there was plenty of time left. He could write quickly when a deadline was near. He was slightly upset when his editor, a woman, called him to ask how he was getting on. He had turned in a synopsis and first chapter to get the advance — what more did they want? They let anyone be editors these days. She asked him out to lunch to talk about the book. That obviously meant she fancied him.

Nigel hedged over an Italian meal. No, he didn't like to disclose too many details about the plot and how much he'd written, but it was going to be really hot. Obviously somebody would want it for a film. He had a film-star second cousin whom he thought could play the role. Nigel knew, of course, that he could have played it better — but acting wasn't a game for gentlemen.

Jo, his editor, had quite fancied him from his photo — most women did. He noticed she went right off him, though, when he said he had expected her to be a man, especially with that name, as she was doing a man's job. She did her duty at the firm's expense, but she was obviously glad when the meal ended. He felt it would have been better manners if she had kept a more friendly or amorous expression throughout.

Nigel's research finally got him into bed with a reasonably good-looking (if not beautiful) woman. He hadn't meant it to go that far, but after nine gins he was anybody's, even a woman's. Much to his disgust he woke with a bad headache in a plebeian bed with a nylon-covered duvet and fitted sheets. The dressing table was kidney-shaped with stencils of roses on it and there was a nylon dressing gown with more roses hanging from a hook on the door. In fact there were bloody roses everywhere, even some real ones (a slightly dead arrangement) on the dressing table. They were cream-coloured and looked left over from a wedding. That really frightened him. Had he committed bigamy while drunk?

When Karen came back smelling of roses, all was explained. 'You'll have to go, darling,' she said. 'I've got to get to work. There are some wreaths to do so I've got to be in early. The other girls don't have my touch.' She helped dress him; he was feeling very delicate, not to mention unappreciated.

'Did we?' he muttered wondering if his breath smelt and making a mental note always to carry a toothbrush.

'Of course, darling!' She kissed him with her hard, pursed mouth and rushed him out of the front door. She went to the left. He stumbled aimlessly to the right. A long walk brought him to Lavender Hill and he hailed a passing taxi cab. As he got in he wondered if he still had his wallet. He checked hastily that everything was still there. It was, together with a card saying:

ROSERAMA
Bouquets for weddings and special occasions

Then he recollected the girl had said she worked in a florist's. He remembered her rough hands on his body with distaste and looked down at his elegant ones only to see that the nails were dirty. He felt and looked thoroughly soiled. He sneaked in quietly, hoping his parents wouldn't notice. His father saw his unshaven appearance and winked at him. He seemed pleased at this evidence of his son's manliness.

Nigel decided to stop going to clubs after that and get down to some serious writing. By four in the afternoon his head had stopped hurting and he did just that. At five-fifteen the phone rang.

'Sweetie, it's your Karen.' She made a horrid kissing sound down the line. 'Haven't you got a kiss for me? You had plenty last night,' she said in hurt tones. He made a faint noise and found he'd spat on the receiver. 'Where are we going tonight, sweetie-pie?' she asked.

'Nowhere. I mean I'm busy tonight – I have another engagement,' he said stiffly. She sobbed in a contrived way. 'Last night was very nice, of course,' he added and, looking at his watch, he lied, 'I have an article to finish, a deadline to meet.'

'Oh yes, you must put your writing first,' Karen said. 'You've got the gift of the gab. I always wanted to meet a real writer.'

At least she was respectful, Nigel thought. He almost began to like Karen as long as she didn't produce those nasty sobbing noises or make a pest of herself. Perhaps he would see her again?

'I've got your number. I'll be in touch,' he said pompously and put the phone down. He placed the card in his desk. Perhaps he could get his mother some flowers cut-price? Karen would surely be willing to do him a favour. His mother's birthday was in a few weeks' time and good flowers are hard to get cheaply in December.

Karen rang him twice in the next week. He was flattered, but slightly perturbed at a woman taking the initiative. He hinted as much to her. He took up her invitation to dinner in her flat and arranged for his cheap flowers. They had a pizza together. He was slightly shocked to see that it was

31

a frozen pepperoni one out of a packet. Really, she could have made more effort for someone like him. The wine was decidedly supermarket, too. He kissed Karen on the sofa, planning to have a headache if she demanded anything more. Much to his relief, she didn't. At least Karen was easy in that department.

When he got home he congratulated himself on his new conquest. She was the kind of mistress he had been looking for. He had had a good night out. He hadn't spent a thing — well, only the bus fare to Clapham — and he had been made to feel like a man again. He ought to do the honourable thing, though, and tell her he was married. Perhaps it could be the subject of a slight quarrel so that he didn't have to buy her a Christmas present.

Everything worked as he intended. He got his flowers for his mother and then quarrelled for Christmas with Karen. About two weeks later, after a comfortable family Christmas with his parents, when the goose and the turkey were long gone and the last of the liqueur chocolates eaten, he phoned Karen and made it up. She was very easy to manage, he decided. Their subsequent night out was not as cheap, though. He had offered her dinner and she had chosen rather an expensive restaurant. She had apologized when she saw the prices, but he said it was all right. He hoped she wouldn't do it again. Everything was patched up nicely. He went home with her, feeling he ought to get his value, but rather dreading it. Part of him was relieved again when she got him to leave after a few kisses. Her sister was staying with her, she said.

The sister seemed to be staying permanently, in fact. Her marriage had broken up and she needed Karen's spare room. He saw Karen about once every two weeks — he didn't want to seem too keen — and always the sister was there. Secretly he was pleased — there was no proving himself or committing himself. He didn't take Karen out again. They just met in her flat and watched telly together. He hoped she would cook for him, and he brought a bottle of wine. Sometimes he was sent out for an Indian takeaway.

Karen was not quite as cost free as she had seemed at first. Still, he was not likely to get a cheaper deal with an unliberated woman elsewhere. Spending a few pounds on someone was decidedly better than having to put up with all that equality shit. A snog from time to time and being thought to have a girlfriend seemed like a very fair trade for a few compliments and the odd vindaloo.

CHAPTER
6

IN THE MONTHS THAT FOLLOWED, NIGEL CONTINUED TO SEE KAREN. Her demands seemed to be growing. He resented having to spend money on her, but she had hinted there was another man who would be glad to be her boyfriend if Nigel didn't take her out. Although Nigel would have been quite happy to lose Karen, he didn't want the ignominy of being dropped for someone else. He tried to think up another quarrel but couldn't find the right excuse.

That summer an excuse came in the shape of a note from Gina. She had a place near Sorrento, she said, and he and Anthony could come and stay as long as they liked. He thought of the sun and the beaches and decided to take time off. He needed peace and quiet to finish the novel. He could afford — just about — to take a break from his freelance work. Perhaps he would stay there for the rest of the summer. He told Karen that he was trying to patch up his marriage. Just to hedge his bets, he hinted that the reconciliation might not work out, and she could wait for him if she liked.

He bought some duty-free perfume on the plane. He could not remember Gina ever wearing any, but it seemed the sort of thing a woman ought to like. He had to look generous with all that free accommodation on offer.

He took the bus from the airport to the main station in Naples, where he boarded a train for Sorrento. It was about an hour's journey. Anthony was old enough to be more of a companion than a nuisance. He had not taken him anywhere when he was younger.

At Sorrento they got a taxi for the last lap. Nigel boasted to his son that he had enough Italian to avoid their being cheated badly. When they arrived at the address Gina had given, it was getting dark. Pensione Brasile was South-American owned and full of seedy types whom Nigel felt sure were terrorists. He asked for Gina in English as there was a notice in the window: *English Spoken.* The fat old woman in black did not understand, so he risked some faltering Italian. After a long interchange of misunderstandings he found out that Gina was working there for the summer as a chambermaid. She had told the proprietor that she would get some English friends to book in and use his hotel. The woman tut-tutted and shook her head when she heard that Nigel was her husband. All he could do was book a room with twin beds for himself and Anthony and ask to see Gina as soon as she was free. He booked in just for the night, not knowing how long he wanted or could afford to stay. The place was scruffy but not cheap.

In about ten minutes Gina came in carrying their sheets. It was swelteringly hot. The first thing she did was tell off Nigel for booking in for only one night. She had been promised commission by the management, she said.

'I told them my English friends would be staying here for the summer.'

'Well, you had a bit of a nerve!' Nigel said faintly as she stormed out of the room.

He and Anthony left the next morning. He didn't see Gina; it was her day off and there was no message from her. When he got to Naples he went straight to the travel office of the company that had issued his plane tickets, which were open-ended. He tried to book for the following day, but was told that the first flight from Naples to Gatwick was not until next week. He decided to pay a little extra and return from Rome in three days' time.

Anthony was glad. He wanted to stay longer. He was proud of his father and liked being away with him. It was the first time they had gone abroad together without Nigel's parents. He was also beginning to be interested in girls. Given several days, he thought he might pick up an Italian who was old enough to teach him a few tricks. One of the boys in his form had boasted of the fun that could be had with an older woman.

The train meandered into Rome by the late afternoon. Nigel felt Rome would be more educational for Anthony — purely in the artistic sense. He had no idea that his fourteen-year-old son had his own plans. He had never really talked to him as an individual. He only spoke to him when he was giving information or telling him to do or not do something. That was his duty, of course.

Nigel found a *pensione* near the station. It was much better, cheaper and cleaner than Gina's place of employment, and they really did speak a little English. The proprietor's wife made much of Anthony, but not in the way he would have liked. She called him Nigel's 'dear little boy'. Anthony assumed that his father was going to get lucky. He was too young to understand about variability in the adult sex-drive. He was still at the age at which boys and girls believe that men are always randy. Anthony began to get more and more annoyed at having his hair ruffled and being dear little boy-ed by the signora. He was determined to go off on his own and prove himself a man.

The next day, threatened with a duty tour of museums and churches, Anthony took off alone. He pinched 20,000 lire from his dad's coat pocket to cover expenses. He thought the beach would be the best place to pick somone up and headed that way. He found from the tourist office that he could get there on the metro. He watched the Italian boys in the crowded carriage rubbing against the girls or putting their hands on their bottoms. He put his hand timidly on the bottom of a Swiss hitchhiker. He felt disappointed that she did not react — perhaps she wasn't able to feel anything through her heavy-duty khaki shorts. He tried an Italian woman in a dress next. She turned and smiled at him, but he saw then that she was middle-aged. He got nervous and moved away. He wanted someone just a little bit older and more experienced than himself. The beach would be the proper place, he decided.

He got off the train at Ostia Lido and followed the crowds.

He was startled to find that you have to pay to go on the beach. He opted to change in the showers as the huts were dearer. If he had had a girl with him he figured the huts would have been worth it for the privacy, but he was beginning to feel unsure that he would find anyone. He looked around him doubtfully at the more developed men. He felt very thin and very white. If he didn't get a girl he would get a tan, he decided. He went and lay down beside two bosomy Italian girls with a transistor blaring pop. One of them sat up and asked him something which he could not understand, so he just said, '*Sono inglese.*' His father had taught him to say he was English in case he got lost. Unfortunately he didn't know anything else. He said his phrase again in reply to the next question and the next. The girls soon realized that these were his only words. One of them gestured to some Italian friends she'd just spotted. They came and listened while she asked a whole string of questions with meanings like 'What do all the wankers say?' or 'What do all the homosexuals say?' The boys joined in with one or two more of their own. Soon, Anthony realized that they were making fun of him. He thought he should go for a swim.

As he had not paid for a beach hut, he had to leave his things on the beach. He left them as far from the group who had been laughing at him as he could. He didn't swim for long. The water was blue but people had dropped a lot of papers in it. He decided he much preferred the grey old English Channel when he could get there on the odd day trip. When he got back to his clothes, he found that most of them were gone. He went across to the girls he'd talked to before but they didn't understand his English and just laughed at him some more.

The thieves had left him his socks and shorts, but very little else. He suspected that they had only left the shorts because they were a little dirty and had a raspberry pop stain on the side. Raspberry pop was a bit of an addiction, although he didn't like to admit this generally. His money had been in a zip pocket in his sweatshirt. That was gone.

His sandals and towel had disappeared, too. He had a ticket for the metro in his shorts' pocket so he decided to head back to the hotel for help.

The pavement was red hot under his feet. He put his socks on in the station while he waited for the train. He had put his shorts on back at the beach. The dampness of his trunks was now working through. A girl on the train pointed out that he looked as if he'd peed himself. Luckily she said it in Italian and he couldn't understand. The rest of the train could, though.

He limped back to his hotel. His big toe had come through one of his tight white socks and the sand inside was rubbing and blistering the soft skin on his feet. His chest, nose and back had turned bright scarlet under the sun.

'*Mamma mia!*' the proprietress said as she handed him his key. When he got upstairs Nigel really told him off. On finding that his son did not have the money he had taken, he was furious. Then he realized he could probably claim it on their insurance if they reported the theft to the police.

Anthony cold-showered for half an hour trying to take the heat out of his burns, then plastered them with calamine. Nigel had borrowed some from Karen's bathroom cabinet before he came on holiday. He figured that he would need it more than her as he had fairer skin and she was just staying in London for the rest of the summer. He ordered Anthony to remove the calamine from his nose before they went to the English-speaking division of the Rome police. 'I'm ashamed of you,' he said. Anthony was chastened and uncomfortable. All thoughts of picking up girls had vanished from his mind. He prayed that no one would put their arm round him or brush against him in the bus.

When they got back, Nigel wrote out an exaggerated claim for his son's sandals and shirt – they had been on their last legs, anyway. He felt better now. At least that meant he would have some cash when he got home. It would have been worse if his son had just spent the money, and the shirt and sandals had fallen apart by themselves.

The rest of Anthony's short stay was very quiet and

educational. He submitted to museums and churches and his feet got even more blistered. Nigel, with the luck of misers, had picked the one Sunday of the month when the Vatican threw its doors open for nothing. It was an exceptionally long morning for a boy who hated and knew nothing about art. The newly cleaned Michelangelos of the Sistine Chapel meant nothing to him because he had never seen the dimmer-coloured dirty ones even in reproductions. He slightly preferred sculptures and looked hard at all the tits of the female goddesses, but decided he didn't find marble ones erotic. It was the texture, or rather what he imagined to be the texture, of real ones that he was interested in. His only consolation amongst all these wonders was knowing that he could boast about having visited them when he got back to school, and gain points with those among his teachers who were culture snobs and hadn't approved of his holidaying in England. He visualized writing essays about Italy and felt even more sick. He could feel his shoulders itching and peeling under his scratchy cotton shirt. He was glad when his father suggested lunch.

They ate spaghetti in a touristy restaurant, more or less opposite, which had the dubious recommendation of large blow-up photos of Kennedy and Nixon with vast piles of the stuff in front of them, large forkfuls on the way to their open mouths. The restaurant was full of Americans.

On Monday they visited a few churches. Nigel had decided museums weren't worth paying for as Anthony was obviously not all that interested. Most of the churches could be looked over free as long as you ignored the priests standing in the aisle with plates. They bussed between them free, also. Nigel taught Anthony not to put his ticket in the machine but to keep it for the next journey. 'Most Italians do that. When in Rome, do as the Romans do,' he said.

In the late afternoon they went to catch their plane. It had been a very short holiday. Anthony hinted he would like to stay on, but his father didn't seem to hear. The plane was small and decrepit and dripped condensation on them. They were sitting next to one of those clever dicks who boasts of working in an airport and says that this might be the plane he didn't quite finish servicing last week or the one he advised his bosses to send to the knacker's yard. They survived their bumpy ride, however. Nigel rang his mother from the airport, which was cheaper than doing it from abroad. It was evening now so it would be cheap rate, too. They'd be home in an hour or so.

On the bus from Victoria, Nigel patted his son's hand and said, 'We won't mention to your gran about anything bad happening, will we?'

'OK, Dad,' Anthony said, assuming he meant the loss of the money.

Mrs Hughes was not altogether surprised that they were home early. She had never liked her son's marriage. She often said that bad marriages should be knocked on the head and not given endless second chances. Perhaps, at last, he could be made to see this and helped to a new start in life with someone who appreciated his intelligence and refinement.

'I say, Liz,' Anthony said to his grandmother, 'guess what Mummy's doing for a living. She's a chambermaid in this foul hotel in Sorrento. Dad said it looked like a brothel for sailors. It was really filthy. He thought terrorists were hiding out there, too, because they were South American. We didn't find any bombs or anything.'

His gran registered the details with pleasure. She was too wise to say 'I could have told you so' – she just saw that they were fed and that Anthony's blisters were taken care of, and she got what snippets of information she could by roundabout questioning.

'You said you wouldn't tell!' Nigel said to Anthony when she went out of the room. 'That's the last time I take you anywhere.'

IT WAS KAREN'S BIRTHDAY NEXT WEEK. HE HADN'T MEANT TO REMEMBER it after she'd dropped so many coarse hints. On the other hand, he still had the duty-free perfume he had bought for Gina and his mother's birthday wasn't till December. He decided to do the generous thing. He hoped she wouldn't think it set a precedent. He would probably have quarrelled with her by next year, anyway. As he was bringing perfume he wouldn't take wine. He didn't want to risk spoiling her.

He knocked at her door on spec and she answered looking rather annoyed, dressed in her rose-covered dressing gown and with a towel wrapped round her head. Her face was clear of make-up and he could see that she had a few spots on her chin. He decided to be charitable. Spots can happen to anyone. He'd even had some once when he was at school.

'You thought I'd forgotten,' he said. 'Here's a little birthday present for my Karen.'

She seemed pleased and went into the kitchen to make them some coffee. He said he needed to pee, in order to return the half-used bottle of calamine lotion. So that it sounded genuine, he left the water running as he fumbled through her bathroom cabinet. He saw with digust that she had lens solution, which must mean she wore contact lenses. He had never noticed, but then he supposed he hadn't really looked into her eyes often. He couldn't quite recollect what colour they were. He remembered them being rather pale like a fish's. He noticed all sorts of other things in the cabinet: Honey Blonde Hiltone, contraceptive pills and tranquillizers, plus lots of make-up. He realized she would be expensive to keep. He preferred girls who had natural good looks and didn't need all that rubbish. He had often hinted to those he had gone out with that they should throw it all away, it only harmed the skin. Curiously though, he never picked the girls who had thrown it all away or who never wore any.

He pulled all Karen's bottles and tubes out and tucked the calamine at the back. He put everything away systematically, then disordered it to make it look the way it had before. The cabinet was overfull and he had difficulty shutting the doors again.

He turned off the tap, pulled the chain and came out of the bathroom. 'Karen?' he said. He went through her Oxfam bamboo curtain into the kitchen. She had put two steaming mugs of coffee on a tray. The mugs were covered in red hearts and there were chocolate-chip cookies on a plate beside them. He ate one of the cookies but decided he didn't like the margariney taste. He carried the tray out into the lounge and put it on a little coffee table by the sofa bed. He turned on the television for a minute, but it was some pop programme. He hadn't really enjoyed memorizing the names of all the hits to impress the girls he'd gone out with. Now he didn't have to bother. Karen was easy to manage. He could hear her in the bedroom blow-drying her hair. He sat and drummed his fingers on the edge of the tray.

When she came out, her face had turned red with the heat, camouflaging her spots. She looked prettier now. She was wearing a little blue eyeshadow. She liked blue because she thought it brought out the blue in her eyes. She had probably read in *Woman's Own* that it was the thing to wear. She had sprayed the perfume liberally on herself. He started to sneeze.

'Got a cold, love?' she asked.

They sipped their coffee and she ate the rest of the biscuits. 'You're going to have to go, love,' she said. 'My sister's old man's coming round. We need to talk as a family. He'll probably crash on the sofa tonight.'

Nigel didn't see why he had to go. He felt a little cheated

after he'd given her perfume. A chocolate biscuit and a mug of instant didn't seem like a fair return. He felt one of her breasts through the nylon and kissed her. She giggled.

'No, honestly, I've got to get my make-up on.'

He sat and watched as she put blobs on her face from a thick pan-stick, then smoothed it out to an even beige. She dusted a brick-coloured blusher below her cheekbones and on her forehead and chin. He thought of the spots again. Then she drew round her mouth with a crayon and filled it in with rose-pink lip gloss. She was applying blue mascara thickly to her lashes as the door chimes rang.

'There now, you'll have to go. Will you be a love and let him in on your way out?'

There was a man at the door, but no sign of the sister. He looked too young to be anybody's 'old man'. Nigel let him in and left. Karen wouldn't lie to him, surely? He had been surprised, though, when he saw the pills in her cabinet. They had only had sex twice and on both occasions he had been too drunk to remember anything in detail. He thought he must have worn a condom, because he'd found a used one sticking to the bottom of his pocket. Perhaps Karen had gone on the Pill just for him. That must be the answer. She must have done it while he was away, so as not to lose him. He wished she had been less liberated and consulted him, but he was prepared to accept it as a loving gesture. He would ring her next week.

CHAPTER

8

ANTHONY KNEW ABOUT KAREN, OF COURSE. HE KNEW THAT SHE WAS a sort of girlfriend of his father's, but he had begun to ask awkward things like, 'Do you fuck her, Dad?'

Dad answered illuminatingly, 'What do you think? You ought to know better than to ask a *man* questions like that.' He emphasized the word 'man' so significantly that Anthony assumed that he did. He hadn't met her but he also assumed she must be pretty, beautiful even. He believed his father deserved that as a man of the world. He himself wanted someone beautiful to fuck and hinted as much to his grandparents. They told Nigel he should be told the facts of life, or rather the ones he hadn't already learnt at school. The sex lesson consisted of Anthony's being told that he was far too young to do it legally, that it wasn't all it was cracked up to be, and that women were dirty so he ought to use condoms.

'What are condoms, Dad?' Anthony asked. 'Are they short for condominiums?' He wanted to imitate the boy he admired most at school. Sam, the son of a butcher, had been overfed on underdone meat like troops before a battle, and had reached a state of simmering lust and heavy manhood by the ripe age of ten. He was always wanking in the school lavs. He was a bit of an oddity, because as well as a long cock he sported slight breasts. The school doctor had told him to slim before he tried any other treatment for these, but hinted that they might have something to do with the hormones used in modern meat production. Sam's father had muttered, 'Bloody vegetarians with their alternative medicine!' and had taken his son home for a slap-up meal.

Sam had been Anthony's chief source of sex education

both in primary and grammar school. The other boys looked up to him. He was bigger, cruder, more assured and more moneyed than all the rest. His father had worked up to owning a huge national chain of butchers' shops. He had cornered the market in several specific cuts of meat for freezers. His shops had got away from old-fashioned butchery — 'Shall I chine it for you, Madam?' — and sold things like four-pound packs of bacon off-cuts, seven-pound sacks of turkey drumsticks and millions of polystyrene trays of chicken breasts, specially boned for chicken Kiev by the women in his factories. 'Men for carrying and chopping, women for tricky little cuts, plucking, gutting and stuffing,' was Sam's father's rule of employment. Yet even he was often appalled by his son's open questions. Sam always delighted his friends with stories of exchanges between father and son.

Nigel was slightly more open with Anthony and less shockable. He just didn't enjoy talking to his son much, so he tried to get shut of subjects quickly. 'Condoms?' he said. 'No, I don't think there's any connection with condominiums — not even an etymological one. Condominium comes from the Latin for joint control. I can't imagine the other things have anything to do with that. Perhaps they come from the name of the bloke who invented them. I'll look it up some time.'

'Yes, but what *are* they, Daddy?' Anthony knew all about them, of course, but he wanted to embarrass his father.

'Oh yes, of course, you want to know what they look like. They're those nasty, wet, rubber things you get on your boot at bus-stops — you know, the ones that stick to you like chewing gum.'

'Should I pick some up next time I go to a bus-stop?' Anthony asked. He'd decided to play along with the adult game.

Nigel could see he would have to demonstrate, even if he wasted one in the process. He pulled one carefully out of the packet and inserted his slim little finger half into it. If his nail didn't go through he would probably be able to use it. 'Here, look,' he said. 'You buy them from chemists or barbers or sometimes slot-machines in lavatories. You put them on like this. Some immoral women even help a bloke to do it. Don't let them do that to you, though. Most of them have long fingernails.'

Anthony could feel the slight dawnings of an erection at the thought of immoral women with long fingernails putting one of those on him, but he couldn't afford to get thoroughly aroused when he was with his father. He was afraid his father might notice him sticking out while they were talking about things like that. He tried to remember his sorrow for his pet newt, Nebuchadnezzar. Nebuchadnezzar had been eaten by a passing gull because Anthony's mother had poured all the jars containing his tadpoles and the newt on to the bird table in the hot sun. He didn't care much about the tadpoles. He was only being dutifully scientific, as his school had told him to. The newt, though, he had liked. It had a bit of personality. At times he thought he had seen it smile.

When Anthony was back to normal he asked his father if he could keep the condom to show the boys at school.

'I think not,' Nigel said, carefully crumpling it back into its foil square and then putting it away with its fellows in a little cardboard box. He pocketed the box casually. 'You know you'll get expelled if you go flashing things like this round. We don't want you having to change schools at a vital stage in your education.'

Anthony vowed to buy himself a pack next time he had his hair trimmed. He didn't like chemists' shops, where he might have to ask a girl for them — one with long nails, who could see what he was thinking.

Nigel walked away. The explanation was at an end and Anthony seemed satisfied. He decided that a visit to Karen might be on the cards while he had that delicate object half in half out of the pack. By tomorrow it would certainly disintegrate.

CHAPTER
9

THE NIGEL–KAREN AFFAIR, IF IT COULD BE CALLED THAT, LASTED UNTIL long after Gina's return. There was no reason for Nigel to drop Karen, or Karen to drop Nigel, because they impinged on each other's lives so little. There was simply nothing worth quarrelling about.

Gina returned in the autumn, heavily tanned. She had quit her job in Sorrento. She came banging on Nigel's door one night. She was now living all on her own in a flat the other side of London, she told him.

'What do you want?' he said stiffly.

'Money,' was the honest answer. He left her a fiver. It was all he intended to spend, or rather lose, for the moment. There was food and drink in the kitchen, he said. He had to go out. She was beginning to look a little faded, he thought. He couldn't quite decide whether the blond streaks in her hair were the effects of the sun or just a bad attempt at covering up grey hairs. He didn't like women once they'd turned thirty. Besides, she was older than him by a few months. He could undoubtedly do better for himself.

He went out on principle to prove he had a life of his own. Anthony was upstairs with his homework. Gina could always do the womanly thing and go and see her son. The only problem was where to go once he'd gone out. He didn't feel like honouring Karen with a second visit that week, so he just wandered off aimlessly and caught a number 19 to the area he worked in. His colleagues all drank at the Coach and Horses or at the Bar Italia. The Coach and Horses was a fairer bet, he thought. It was nearer and also people there were less inclined to knock back the Pernods. If he went fairly late, it was extremely likely that someone would offer him a drink. He could always leave before it was time for him to buy a round. He would ask for something modest like white wine, so that he was not really expected to buy. As a creative writer he felt he had a certain natural right to such perks. Only those with boring, regular jobs needed to pay their way.

His editor bought him a drink and all went well. The man who wrote the art column had a private-view card for an exhibition in Smith's Gallery in Earlham Street. Nigel wasn't much interested in paintings and he was slightly frightened of the art critic because he was gay. He often assumed that all homosexuals were out to jump on every other man, ignoring the fact that many of them had relationships far more stable than his. Would he be safe with his colleague, he wondered? On the other hand, going to the exhibition would mean more free drink, some food perhaps – peanuts if nothing else – and another hour wasted to show Gina who was boss.

At the gallery, he met an old school friend who worked for a literary magazine. Charles was a dedicated male chauvinist and hinted that he would like Nigel to write a regular article. 'We *real* men must stick together,' he said loudly, turning his back on the art critic.

By the fourth free glass of wine, Nigel began to feel kindly to everybody. 'He's a bit of a bugger but I quite like him!' he said, sniggering, and pointed to the critic. Then he remembered he'd left his wife at home. 'Good old Gina, she brought me luck today. I've got a new job, you know!' he told his friend who'd just given him one, seizing him by the lapels.

Charles and the critic shovelled Nigel into a taxi and Charles went with him. For a moment he thought it was the critic. 'I know,' he said playfully, 'you're after my body. Well, you can't have it – it's someone else's – my wife's, I mean.'

Drunks are usually forgiven a lot. Charles was going to insist on Nigel's taking the taxi to his door, but Nigel decided he'd rather be left at South Kensington. He had just enough sense in him to remember that he didn't have much money. If he was dropped a few blocks from home, he knew Charles would be last out and therefore have to pay. His friend lived in Chelsea — the other side of the King's Road. He had checked up on that.

'I need a little walk,' he said. 'Got to sober up before I see the missus, you know.' There was no arguing with that.

When he got home, everything was dark, so he went round to the back. She would be in the kitchen most probably. He thought he might show his appreciation to Gina tonight, even if she did look a bit faded. After all, he had left her a fiver and fivers don't grow on trees. He went round the back and in through the kitchen door, which had been left ajar. There was no Gina. He whistled softly and a man rushed by him and out into the night. Nigel was really worried then. Perhaps she had been assaulted? How would it look to the police that he wasn't there at the time? If it was serious, at least he'd have an alibi, though. He went through the house, turning on lights wherever he could. A few papers were scattered around, but he couldn't see anything of importance missing. He was not sure about small things, because his parents were away for a couple of days celebrating their fortieth anniversary. Only his mother would know the contents of all the drawers.

Upstairs, Anthony was watching telly, his homework still undone. He was completely unaware of any disturbance, or that Gina had been and gone. Someone at school had told him disco dancing would give him more muscles, and also that women liked men who danced well. So he used to turn the music up full blast when he was alone with the television or record player. He would step to the left for one beat, then to the right, put one fist forward, then the other. Sometimes he'd revolve slowly. It didn't look quite right in the mirror, but he was working on it.

'You watch too much of that crap,' Nigel said when he came in and turned it off. 'You'll never be a fine writer with two good jobs and two women after you, like your father.'

'You're pissed, Dad,' Anthony said admiringly.

CHAPTER
10

GINA KEPT AWAY FOR A WHILE AFTER THAT VISIT. NIGEL WENT ON WITH his life. His new job brought him more money and enabled him to finish his novel. He had gone way past the delivery date in writing it, so the last few months were fraught with anxiety. He pushed his luck to the stage where the publishers were starting to ask for their money back, then he made frantic attempts to deliver. The whole thing had to be retyped first. He hoped Karen would do some of it for him. She had, after all, once told him she was not just a common florist: she had office skills as well.

Karen did not possess a typewriter so he took his portable round. He even offered to make coffee while she got started. As he was spooning the instant into the heart-covered mugs they always used, he heard hesitant taps coming from the other room. He began to realize he had made a mistake.

'You've got it all wrong, darling,' he said as he handed her the coffee. She put it down immediately on his typescript, leaving a ring. 'You can't type a manuscript on coloured notepaper – especially one that smells of roses. That perfume's all very nice on you, dear, but my editor wouldn't appreciate it. She'd think I was a poofter or something.'

'Your editor's a woman!' Karen said, wide-eyed with disbelief. 'But you told me you worked for a man.'

'So I do,' Nigel said. 'That's at the office. This is something else. You see, when you send work to a publisher, that's different. Their names may look very male in the *Writers' and Artists' Yearbook*, but that doesn't necessarily mean anything. It doesn't tell you who's going to edit you – sometimes it's a woman.'

'Oh, I see,' she said, but didn't.

'Well, could my Karen do a little better for me if I brought a block of nice white A4 from the office?'

The nice white A4 was brought and Karen set out to ruin her weekend. He left her to it as he didn't want to hang around doing nothing or waiting on her. He turned up at one o'clock on Sunday to take her to lunch. She had got through most of the paper and most of the weekend doing a passable first chapter. When she went wrong she started a fresh sheet, as she had never heard of Tipp-Ex. He took pity on her, saying what she'd done was enough, and put the remainder of the paper in his briefcase to take home. Now he had to give her the promised lunch. He delayed a little. The nearby pub always ran out of roast meat by one-thirty and you had to content yourself with cheese rolls after that. A cheese roll and a lager was fair enough payment for Karen's level of 'office skills'.

Nigel took back his portable and did the second chapter that night at home. Perhaps one of the office girls would help him out. He must remember to be nicer to them.

He took his article in a little late next day. What with typing that and the second chapter of his book he was falling behind schedule. He must now scout around for a suitable female candidate to type his book. There were several secretaries and young literary dogsbodies working for the weekly review magazine that he had just started on. Secretaries were more money-conscious, he decided, so someone pea-brained with unsuccessful literary aspirations would be a safer bet. That left him with a choice of three. Two were shaky typists like him. The really efficient one was a feminist, unfortunately. Perhaps he could spread the load and try and exploit more than one at once.

Isobel might be the safest bet, he decided. She had a very low, large bosom and long black hair. She fawned over all the men in the room to such an extent that they began to mistrust any attraction they might have otherwise felt. They used to discuss her in the gents. 'God, she must be desperate! She held *my* hand, hugged *you*, kissed old so-and-so on his bald pate – and that was only the first five minutes.' Multiple flirting seldom reaches any target. Isobel certainly was desperate.

'I've just finished my masterpiece,' Nigel declared.

Isobel gave a whoop and kissed and hugged him. 'Hey, that's great,' she said. 'Can I read it?'

'Well, I can hardly read it myself, that's the only trouble. Got to get it all retyped by the end of the month or my publisher'll dump me. I can't give you the whole thing to read as I need it to type from. My other copy is *really* unreadable. Ah, if only I had a team of secretaries. I would *really* love for you to be the first to read this. I've always valued your opinion a lot.'

Isobel genuinely wanted to help, but she was a busy woman. She was the literary editor and he was just a freelance. She got one of the secretaries to put the lot through the photocopier and took it home. At least Nigel now had a second copy of the first two chapters and another battered typescript to play with. His publisher's contract demanded two copies. He was a little further along the line.

'Look, Isobel,' he said. 'Could you do me an even bigger favour? Could you possibly retype chapter three tonight? I'm asking you for a very special reason – I was thinking of you when I wrote that chapter – you'll notice the girl in it's a brunette. I can't bear to retype that bit myself.'

Isobel agreed, of course. Maybe he'd have to pay her more attention in future but it was a small price for having a little more of his manuscript completed. He could always act the pious married man if she got too serious later.

'If you can leave it all for me at the reception desk tomorrow,' he said, 'you'll have saved my life. I don't know what time I'll be passing, so it would be better left there. Sometime we'll meet when we can be alone together and discuss it, and *everything*.'

Nigel felt safe with the mention of them being alone. He knew Isobel was too busy for that. She blushed and looked properly thrilled at her task. He went on to the other magazine he worked for. It was not his day for bringing in an article, so this visit was more social. He got a coffee from the editor's secretary. He had gone in the lunch hour knowing that his boss would be out of the way and she would be alone with her carton of plain yoghourt and fruit. She was trying to slim. He sipped his coffee and accepted half her grapefruit. Then Mrs Honeywood was duly persuaded to do one chapter for him while he used the photocopier to make a rough copy of the rest. A couple more chapters were farmed out to other co-workers on the Isobel technique. He made sure that they were freelances who did not know each other too well. He swore them to secrecy over their connection with the characters in the book.

By the end of the week he had six chapters typed by different women and four by himself, plus various photocopies to work from. He was roughly halfway through. He sent the first part of his book to the publisher, explaining that the rest would follow in a few weeks. He blamed the typists for their slowness. 'I'm sure you will understand and will have had similar problems', he finished his letter.

He was out of favours now, so it looked as if he would have to pay for the rest if he wanted it quickly. Perhaps, though, there might be a way to get it done cheaply. . . . The feminist on the review mag was said to be setting up a typing agency from home in the evenings. Perhaps she could be persuaded. Jude hated dealing with men so Nigel decided to ask Isobel to approach her. Isobel had shown she had good taste by including a postcard of Michelangelo's David with the manuscript when she left it at reception. On the back she had written *Great!*

He persuaded Isobel to say that the last half of the manuscript was her own. Jude, like a good feminist, gave forty per cent discounts to women. Isobel explained that she had taken a male, sexist persona for her first novel. Jude delivered the work quickly. She was glad of an opportunity to show her efficiency. It was done cheaply in a few days by the unmarried mothers and battered wives to whom she farmed out work.

'I only read a chapter or two of your book,' she said to Isobel. 'My God, your alter ego's a conceited prat. Don't ever have a sex change. I prefer you the way you are.'

CHAPTER
11

JO, NIGEL'S EDITOR, SEEMED HAPPY ENOUGH WITH THE FINISHED NOVEL. At least, she was pleased that it was finished. She recognized it was exactly what had been commissioned by her bosses. She knew Nigel was no male Jane Austen. Subtlety was not his forte. She hinted he might have overestimated the book's film possibilities. In film terms it fell between two stools, she said. The scenario suggested a kind of up-market *Confessions of a Window Cleaner*. On the other hand *Confessions of a Window Cleaner* had an ideological advantage over Nigel's book in that Mr Ordinary could more easily identify with a window cleaner than with a literary gent getting a leg over.

Although Nigel had said proudly that the book was loosely autobiographical, Jo believed it to be more of a fantasy creation. The sex scenes were described in porno-mag terms. The women were always panting for it and crying out for more when he jumped on them, not to mention telling him he was wonderful afterwards. Nothing ever seemed to go wrong. There were no refusals, no collapsing condoms, no impotence. Everything was far less like life than she would have liked. Still, there was no doubt that the novel would sell adequately, if not wonderfully. She could see that a few thousand was probably the top whack, but that was all right for a first novel. Most of Nigel's friends were male reviewers. He was sure of a few good mentions. She made a mental note to tell the publicity people to avoid sending the book to women's magazines or the left-wing sort of papers.

Nigel felt strangely flat once his book was finished. There was some editing to do, then there would be the proofs in a few months' time, but it felt like a thing of the past. He looked forward to the publicity in about nine months, though, when the book was scheduled to come out. He envisaged glamour photos of himself on the covers of magazines. Perhaps he would strike it really big.

For the moment there were just life's usual problems. Gina was in touch occasionally by telephone. She didn't have much to say. He felt she was only checking up to see that he was still with his parents and still alone. Karen was getting a shade possessive, now she thought he was famous and therefore a good catch. She hinted at divorce several times, but he simply said it was out of the question. She also had had the bad taste to ask him how much his advance was. It sounded like a lot of money to her.

'People in ordinary jobs often think of advances as a kind of pools win,' Nigel tried to explain. 'They're not like that, though. They usually come in three parts – one for the idea, one for the finished manuscript and the other on publication.They're really an author's salary, except that he gets some of it in advance. I'll have to budget and make this money last until the next book, whenever that is. You see I don't really have enough money for a holiday or anything like that. If you like, we can go for a celebration drink and perhaps a Chinese, too, when the book's actually out.'

Karen said that she was beginning to have doubts about Nigel's suitability as a boyfriend. He sat on her sofa, listening in amazement as her feelings spilled out. Her life was slipping by, she said. She had got very little out of their relationship. If she could marry him it would be a step up, and his foibles would be worth putting up with. On the other hand, he was a few years older, very much married already and she was sick of his meanness. She was nearing thirty, getting a few grey hairs. If there was no action soon, she could end up with no marriage and no kids. Someone younger, though commoner, might well be a safer bet and would definitely be more highly sexed. Almost anyone was. She didn't fancy Nigel all that much physically – he was older than her and very different in looks. Even so, she was slightly offended by his lack of desire. She didn't want him when she was sober, but she would have liked to have had to fend him off. She wasn't going to chase after him again and from now on she would be seeing more of other men.

Nigel distanced himself for a while after that. He had his own problems. He had laid these up for himself when he farmed out several chapters of his typing. He now had three women who thought they were in the book and that he owed them a favour. He tried changing the times he called in at the two magazines for which he wrote pieces, but they always seemed to be there. The two freelances now had permanent jobs and were homing in on him. He couldn't escape them. It was enough to make a braver man cringe. The idea of being in demand had been nicer than the reality.

Isobel seemed to be the biggest problem of all. She never took a day or even an hour off. She was a workaholic. She was always there whenever he went in to deliver articles, waiting to put her hands all over him. She still kissed the bald editor on his pate, she still hugged his friend, but Nigel came in for a double ration of everything. She often came up behind him by the coffee maker and put her arms around him, pressing her breasts into him. She was so short that they only came up to the small of his back. Or if he was sitting down, she'd blindfold his eyes with her hands and say, 'Guess who?', leaning forward so that a swathe of hair brushed his cheek. He could see a few specks of dandruff cascading down on to the table. Once some went in his coffee.

'Here, have mine,' he said, handing it to her.

'How romantic,' she said, 'sharing the same cup.'

Frequently the gents was his only refuge. Sometimes he'd beckon Charles in after him for a chat. He knew it could not harm his own reputation. After all, when his book came out, he would be known as a successful womanizer. 'I have this nightmare,' he told his friend. 'I have this awful, awful nightmare of being smothered by her huge greasy tits – and then being talked to death afterwards.'

He began to get severe nausea at the sight of Isobel. Mentally he compared the feelings she aroused in him to the time he ate two whole candy flosses and had a ride on the dodgems on the Isle of Wight at the age of eleven. He had had a girlfriend then who was seven and had ordered him to pick her a bucketful of winkles off some slimy rocks to the peril of his life. He couldn't remember her name, but he had really loved her. She was very exploitative, nearly as bad as Gina, but prettier. The candy flosses had been a bout of mistaken compulsive eating on his way home to compensate for losing her. He could still recall the awful spun sugar sticking to the end of his nose and its flavour combining with that of the metal of the dodgem controls when he'd tried to lick his fingers clean.

He began to plan timid insults to make Isobel take the hint and piss off. 'I don't like pushy women,' he told her one day while she had her arm round his back, her hand nonchalantly sliding towards his right buttock.

'I can't stand them either,' she said. 'I much prefer to have men working under me. I've always been like that.'

CHAPTER
12

IN THE END, NIGEL DECIDED THAT THE ONLY EFFECTIVE DETERRENT to Isobel would be the sight of him with another woman. He was not all that proud of Karen — he seldom took her anywhere — but she might be his only hope. Alternatively, he could let Isobel see him with one of the women on the *Left Arts Review*, the other magazine he wrote for. That might work better as they were fellow professionals.

There was Nina. She had hair like a lion's mane and a very beaky nose. She was not everyone's cup of tea, although she was said to appeal to the odd masochist. Fran, who usually wrote the end piece in the magazine, seemed like a more suitable candidate. She had shoulder-length, dyed blond hair, a curly easy-care perm, a dark tan and usually wore denim. She might pass for glamorous by most people's standards, he decided. By his exacting standards, she did not. After all, she openly admitted to being thirty-six — a few months older than he was. He hated, too, her annoying habit of wearing sunglasses in her hair even in winter. She used the damn things as a sort of Alice band to keep the frizz back. She was the exact physical opposite of Isobel, too — taller, thinner, flatter, fairer. If Isobel saw her she might infer that in real life, if not in books, he only fancied blondes.

He didn't like Fran's column much. She tried too hard. She always had to mention condoms or pills or thrush or something, just to show she was with it. In his view she handled sex grossly in her writing. There was no romance. At least she didn't paw him like Isobel, though. The worst he could expect from her was a straight verbal pass. You can stay friendly with people after those.

Fran was invited for a lunch-time drink at a pub near the

magazine he worked on with Isobel, the *London Literary Times*. As they were nearing the pub he mentioned having to deliver his weekly article and invited Fran to come up with him. 'It'll only take five minutes,' he said. 'The editor usually laps my work up.'

He made Fran and himself a coffee while he waited for Isobel's verdict. Isobel edited the pages he wrote for. He would have liked to have had male editors only, but there seemed to be fewer and fewer choices in his life lately. As he grew older he saw younger women passing him in the promotion stakes. He comforted himself that editing was just a job, they weren't *real* writers. On the other hand, he had to admit that some of them wrote novels as well. Of course, their novels weren't as promising as his.

Isobel hung on his arm and told Fran that they were close friends. Then she reminded him to put money in the office tin for the coffee he'd made for himself and 'whoever she is'. She held the tin out until he had scraped a few bob in change from his pocket. She was decidedly less effusive about his column than usual, too. The last few she had let through verbatim even though they were slightly over length. There were notes about the contributors beneath his column and these could be shortened easily enough, or the odd less important name left off. Nigel was so used to getting away with a hundred words over that he had not bothered to count. As long as it filled up three and a half sheets of A4 he felt it would be right.

Isobel sat down and counted loudly, marking down numbers beside the paragraphs with a blue biro. Nigel stood by amazed. He wasn't used to this treatment. Usually she just stood and chuckled, pawed him a little and said, 'That's great!'

When she'd totted up the numbers and checked her arithmetic she told him the piece wouldn't do. It was ninety words over. 'I don't have the time at the moment to edit it,' she went on. 'Look, Jonjon's typewriter's lying idle. He's gone to the VD clinic for a blood test. Thinks he's got something again. Use that. This typescript's a bit too messy with the numbers down it. Get it sorted out while I'm at lunch. I'll be back round about two.'

Fran left shortly after. 'I think we'd better take a rain check on the drink,' she said tactfully.

Nigel got his piece done, then went and washed his hands thoroughly. He was slightly afraid the typewriter might carry germs. Isobel came back at two, but had to make a few phone calls before she could get down to business. The final column was passed, although she decided to change a few paragraphs round. It made very little difference to the sense, Nigel thought.

The next week Nigel counted his piece immaculately before he took it in. He pencilled the exact number of words at the top to avoid a repetition of his previous treatment. Isobel read it coldly without a smile on her face. He didn't bother with coffee — it wasn't worth paying for. There were no chuckles. He resented that. He had assumed they were involuntary — brought on by the wit of his writing.

'Yes. Thank you,' she said. 'I'm afraid you'll have to excuse me, Nigel. I have rather a lot of work to do.' She pinched his bum viciously as she went back to her desk.

That was in very poor taste, Nigel thought. He went into the gents, muttering, 'I bet the bitch has bruised me.' He stood on the hot pipes opposite the mirrors over the washbasins. By standing on tiptoe on one leg and dropping his trousers he could just about see his left buttock. It seemed only to be slightly reddened. He was taken back to his old schooldays when he had last dropped his trousers to examine the damage. Jonjon came in at that moment, fresh from the VD clinic, but looking cheerful.

'Hey, what's up with you, old man?' he said. 'You haven't been to the "naughty spanker" advertised in Mr Patel's window on the corner, have you?'

Nigel scrambled his trousers up quickly in embarrassment. 'Just a boil coming up,' he muttered, 'but don't tell the others.' He knew it was useless to say that. Jonjon told everybody everything. He couldn't even keep his VD to himself. On the last occasion he'd come in boasting,

'Cracker of a nurse took my sample. Made a date for next month when I'm cured.' He had rattled his bottle of pills dramatically. 'She can have me right after I've been for my next test. Certified germ-free — what more could a young girl ask?'

Nigel kicked himself for being seen with his pants down and saying it was a boil. Since he'd been caught, he wished he'd at least had the sense to drop Isobel into the office gossip. He sneaked in very early the next Monday to leave his column. He kept several feet from his editor as she read glumly. As she moved towards him he moved away. It was over soon enough with exactly the same words as last week. He thought he'd got off lightly. Downstairs, the doorman stopped him.

'You're Nigel Griffiths?'

'No, Hughes.' Nigel was annoyed. The man ought to know who he was by now.

'Ah yes, that's the name. I knew it was something Welshy. Right, I've got a present for you.' He handed it over the counter with a smirk. Some joker had left him a gift-wrapped rubber ring and a get-well card — 'Are you sitting comfortably? If not, you will be now. From your pals in the office.'

'Bloody women,' he muttered. On the way home he took it into the local Sue Ryder shop. Moments later he remembered the card was still taped to the package. He went back in. 'There was an envelope with a card in. I left it by mistake attached to that kids' toy I gave you. My Anthony doesn't need it — he's grown up and can swim properly without those things. I'd like the card back, if I may. I left it by mistake.'

'Of course,' the woman said. 'I'm sorry, we were just looking at it.' She was obviously trying not to laugh as she handed it back. He dropped it in the litter bin outside.

Nigel always blamed Isobel for the rubber ring. He blamed her, too, for his losing his job soon after. Maybe he was right, maybe he was wrong. The fact that there was a new editor might also have had something to do with his loss of employment. The bald one had left — perhaps he'd had enough of Isobel. He moved to a Page-Three, tits-and-bums sort of paper. It was an odd transition after a lifetime of more literary journalism, but it seemed to suit the editor. He was frequently seen on television, on quizzes and chat shows. He became a bit of personality once he bought himself a neat, ginger wig. Everybody sussed out it was false and that gave him the recognizability of a caricature. Comics impersonated him in sketches which showed him being scalped by irate royals or by pop stars who'd appeared in his paper. Eventually he was to graduate to *Spitting Image*. Nigel was not so lucky.

CHAPTER
13

THE *LEFT ARTS REVIEW* WAS ALSO TO HAVE A NEW EDITOR SOON. Nigel met him at a party and found him very left indeed and in a humourless way. His predecessor had been much more urbane. Under its new editor the paper began to take on a more socially aware tone and the culture became educational. Nigel feared his new boss's socialism might lead him to sack all those he considered had privileged backgrounds. Nigel couldn't help having been to that sort of school any more than others could help having been part of the state system. He was puzzled as to why some people resented his background.

In many ways he felt underprivileged. He was not getting on as fast as inferior contemporaries. He was not having as much publicity as women writers. He saw the faces of lady novelists grinning at him off festival brochures and newspapers everywhere. 'Look at those tarts – not a set of brains between them!' he'd say to his male colleagues. None of it seemed fair when he was photogenic and took just as much trouble with his shining, blow-dried blond hair. He couldn't imagine even a female film star being as unwrinkled and having such a greyhound-slim body and such thick hair. He didn't have the slightest trace of recession. He felt he would look good in one of the colour supplements.

There is nothing like an inequality between personal merit and job chances for making a person feel put upon. Thirty-five was a turning point at which you could start to be middle-aged, Nigel thought. By that age, his father had been an exceptionally rich man with a settled family life, as had Nigel's brothers, William and David. Nigel had achieved merely a lot of hack articles and a novel. That novel was his only chance. He blessed the fact that his parents' house in Chelsea gave him a millionaire background against which to be photographed, and one which he had not had to earn for himself. But then his father died and his mother didn't wish to keep the house on. Nigel's peace and complacency were shattered. He hadn't entirely loved his father — he'd sensed his disapproval of his life style and choice of wife. Still, he could rely on him. Women couldn't be leant upon in the same way.

Nigel was not a great deal of help to his mother. He showed his resentment when she wanted to pack up and go to her new flat right away. She asked him to move in — it was a large apartment with three bedrooms — but a chance meeting spoiled that for him. Some friend of his mother's who had not seen her since youth had bumped into them when they were lunching in Fortnum's together — her treat. 'Is that your toy-boy, darling?' the friend had asked. 'Very nice! Must be a good ten years younger than us. Does he have a brother?' It cheered his mother up a lot, but Nigel wasn't the same for days. Oh no, he couldn't share a flat with her after that.

They had two months before the person who was buying the house required vacant possession. William organized most of the details through his firm's solicitor. He had always been practical. He took one or two pieces of furniture and Nigel was left with just a few things that his mother didn't want for her Knightsbridge flat. He found a small house in Highgate, not far from his old one. It was slightly tatty Victorian. He still had quite a bit of the capital left from his former days as a house-owner. He hadn't spent much living at home. He needed only a small mortgage to pay off the rest. He pretended to the building-society manager that he still had his second job as a journalist. He thought the employees there might have the decency to cover for him if asked. He probably wouldn't have any difficulty with the mortgage, anyway — more work was bound to turn up as soon as his novel was out. Best of all, he managed to wangle his conveyancing on the general solicitor's bill for the settling of the will and the sale of his parents' house. William paid the whole thing without question.

He kept well away from Karen during this period of his life. He was afraid she might suggest that he move in with her. He knew who'd have to pay the rent then. It would be no life for him, stuck in a shabby flat in Clapham with a romantic florist. He could always pick up with Karen at some future date. He could pretend he'd been devastated by the bereavement. When he did, though, he decided not to let her know that he now had a house of his own. All women were mercenary.

At the same time as his father died he heard from Gina. She said she wanted a divorce. He wrote her a pompous letter, which he had to send to a friend of hers because she wouldn't tell him where she was staying. ('I am moving around. I am a gipsy. We circus stars are.') In the letter he said he would provide her with the requisite evidence. He thought in terms of the days when people played cards all night with a chambermaid in a seedy hotel so that a private eye could photograph them at breakfast.

There was no answer, so some weeks later he followed his letter up with a short note mentioning that he had changed address. He had to give her the new address, of course. That was different, she was his wife. A few days afterwards, Gina was at his door.

'I am back,' she said. 'You are the love of my life and I have nowhere to stay.' She had arrived with a couple of packing cases full of stuff. A friend with a van had dropped her.

Nigel helped her in. 'I don't think you'd better stay if we're getting divorced,' he said. 'It might complicate things. There's a private hotel two streets away. Perhaps I should phone them and see if they have a room for you. You can leave your things here till the morning.'

'My foolish Nigel,' she said. 'We promised to be together in the registry office.' (Nigel didn't remember any *till death us do part, in sickness and in health* bits, but he was flattered and didn't quibble). 'We must keep that promise,' she went on. 'For the child's sake I forgive you . . . everything.'

Nigel wondered what he was being forgiven for, but couldn't kick his wife out as she had nowhere to go. He succumbed to a night of passion instead, or rather, yet another night when she thanked him for trying.

CHAPTER
14

SOON LIFE BECAME VERY MUCH AS IT HAD BEEN BEFORE THEIR separation, except that Gina was a little more violent. Nigel needed more money now he had a mortgage and a wife again, so he started holding workshops in his own home. Often, he had to hide the marks Gina had given him from his pupils. He sat by the window, against the light. He believed they might not be able to see the scratches on his face or the vestiges of a black eye that way. On the other hand, he thought, if they did see them, most of the girls were too tactful to say anything. They all fancied him and would think his wife must be a monster. Gina almost always kept out of the way when he had anyone in. He did the same when she had friends there.

It was a small house so they had to share a bed. Anthony had the other bedroom. Occasionally Gina invited circus friends. If Nigel was there she gave them blankets and told them to use the sofa. They were not as obliging as she was about disappearing before the weekly workshop. Sometimes a pupil would arrive just as one of them was waking up. The girl then had to sit nervously on the edge of the sofa — there weren't many chairs — while the guest stretched himself, yawning, naked and sweaty.

There began to be a great fall-off in attendance. Nigel's lessons were flagging. He was slightly anti-semitic, so he called the girls, who were from an exclusive private school, 'little Jewish princesses' behind their backs. He told his literary friends that their stories and poems were so awful he didn't know what to say about them or how to get through the scheduled hour. Often he made them criticize each other's work. It saved him the effort. On one of these occasions, one of Gina's old friends came in useful. The tattooed man sat up in the middle of the lesson, his blankets draped like a toga and barely concealing 'Jane' and 'King Kong' on his chest. Nigel was flagging, but much to his relief the man took over and delivered an admirable lecture on French surrealist poetry. The pupils thought he'd been brought in specially for their benefit and turned up the next week with more surrealistic pieces. Nigel couldn't stand poetry of any sort – well, perhaps limericks or his own early efforts. Surrealism was definitely the last straw.

Nigel pretended a relative had just died and managed to get out of most of the remaining classes of the term. At first he had liked the thought of bringing in a lot of women to make Gina jealous. The trouble was she didn't seem to care tuppence. He might as well not bother. It was all too much like hard work. He would make the extra money by giving similar classes away from home. Then Gina might worry more about what he was doing. He got a residency for the next year at the University of Kent and spent half the week in Canterbury. He could easily have commuted, but liked the ambiguity of living in two places. He exhorted Gina not to use too much heat or light while he was away.

Every weekend, Anthony was bursting with news for him. Sometimes it was just stuff from school. Other times it was about Gina. 'Mummy had a photographer last week,' he said. 'She told me he'd come to take pictures of her throwing knives in the bedroom. Someone interviewed her for an Italian magazine – they're doing a piece about her family, or so she says. When I looked in your bedroom she had him in there with her and he'd left his camera downstairs. I've taken the film out of it.'

Nigel took the pictures to be developed. Sure enough there were several of Gina throwing knives in their bedroom. She had a target with a blown-up colour photo of him on it. The earlier prints on the film were of men who were being rolled across canvases covered in paint.

'You see, Anthony,' Nigel said. 'You had it all wrong – your mother was just doing her silly act, like these avant-garde artists. It's men who are unfaithful to women, not vice versa. You'll know that when you're a bit older. Women her age usually give up sex — she's a few months older than me, you know. It was a waste of three quid getting these developed, so no more of your bright ideas, messing with people's cameras. I'd probably have had to compensate that bloke if you'd broken it, and professional photographic equipment costs a devil of a lot, you know.'

The next week Nigel was regaled with similar tales. Anthony even claimed to have discovered 'maps of Ireland' on the sheets when he stuffed them into the machine in the local Launderette. When Nigel was at home, Gina usually made him take them to the Launderette in a black dust bag. 'Here are your filthy sheets,' she used to say. He'd put his elbow up slightly as he took the bag from her because sometimes she would clout him with it. It didn't really hurt as long as she didn't get his face. He had the sort of sensitive nose that made him instantly burst into tears if it got the slightest knock.

There were more tales about the photographer in the following months. When he thought about it, Nigel did find it a little odd that a photographer should return after he'd finished a job. He ought to have been off somewhere else on a shoot by now. On the other hand, Gina had assured him that he was doing publicity photographs for her. Why should she bother to lie? Gina was very proud of the photographs. She had an artist friend print up some material for her, using a picture that showed her in profile. She was proud of her long, flexible nose. She had the unusual skill of being able to pull the end down like a tapir when she was angry. (Nigel reckoned she would make an exceptionally good girner when she lost all her teeth.) Soon, her beak was silhouetted on everything — curtains, cushions and upholstery. She didn't sew herself, so she had an acquaintance from a theatrical costumiers run them up in his spare time. It cost rather a lot, Nigel discovered when he looked at the bills he was expected to pay. He agreed to pay them but told Gina she must give some Italian lessons or something in future if she wanted to treat herself to things like that. He had heavy commitments on the house.

Gina did indeed start giving lessons of a kind. Sometimes she would disappear for days. She had a room the other side of London — it was years, though, before Nigel discovered that. When he checked in the new phone book to see that his entry was there he did not, of course, look through all the Hugheses.

When Gina was not smacking him with the laundry bag or scratching his face, they lived a life of complete indifference to one another. That was why he preferred the violence — it showed she felt something for him. He took to picking up pretty young girls just so that he could complain about her. It made it all worthwhile. His technique was to go up to one at a literary party and ask her for a cigarette.

To Nigel's disappointment, nothing ever came of these pick-ups. He often invited the girls back to his house, but most of them came only once. Some piece of rudeness from Gina would put them off. If any of them hinted afterwards that his wife might not be thrilled at seeing them again, he'd say, 'You can tell her to bugger off any time.' But they were the ones who buggered off. If they'd really cared for him, Nigel reasoned, they'd have stayed.

CHAPTER
15

NIGEL HAD NOT SEEN KAREN IN ABOUT SIX MONTHS AND WHEN HE finally called on her she was cold. She had assumed that everything was over. He tried to start things up in a half-hearted sort of way, but she gave him an ultimatum. If there was to be any relationship, she wanted to see his head on the pillow most mornings. She needed someone there. Nigel of course didn't give in to blackmail. He felt she was after entrapping him. She had told him a tale, looking slyly at him while she played with his left hand. 'A friend of mine who's a florist got married the other day and she had a really lovely do and it cost almost nothing. She used the roses from the last wedding she'd handled. She just put a dash of bleach in the water and they came up lovely. And she got all the rest of the stuff cost price because she was used to liaising with the caterers and photographers before other people's weddings. They made an agreement that she would give them her left-over flowers for their shops. Oh, and she got a lovely video made of her wedding day.'

It all sounded so romantic, Nigel nearly threw up. He mistrusted stories about 'friends'. People often say 'a friend' did this when they mean themselves. He'd used the same technique sometimes as a prelude to complaining about his marriage.

Karen went on. 'It's marvellous how good second-hand flowers can be. I often clean them out of the church after the wedding. The brides usually keep their bouquets, or rather whoever caught them does. I caught one at my friend's wedding last week. You know what that means, don't you?' She nudged him meaningfully. 'I was able to sell it again, too, with a renewed frill round the edge. We used to use a sort of doily to go round them, but now you can get washable plastic lace by the yard, which lasts much better. Some miserable registry-office job wanted a bouquet in a hurry. She was getting married in a plain cream suit, too. Can you imagine?'

At least he hadn't had to bother with flowers for Gina. Their wedding, mercifully, had been the sort of rushed job that Karen was busy despising. He began to appreciate his wife a little for her lack of romance and her low cost. No, Karen was definitely getting ideas above her station. He prided himself that he never dropped people − he was too chivalrous for that − on the other hand, if he poked fun at her she would probably drop him.

In practice, however, he found that Karen couldn't be provoked easily. She didn't even notice he was making fun of her. She regularly boasted about not having a sense of humour. If he made a joke and she realized it was one, she used to butt him in the chest − she was much shorter − and say 'You're silly!' For a little while it had amused him. It seemed fresh and charming compared with some of the bawdy, world-weary journalists he had to deal with. They always saw his jokes before he got to the punch line. Yet the thought of being tied to Karen permanently made him sick. Small doses of non-sophistication were amusing as a break from other things, but he wouldn't have been able to bear all that romance day in, day out. Gina was at least unpredictable.

'Only uneducated women who've got nothing else to think about like show-off white weddings,' Nigel said. 'They think having their picture in the paper's everything. I get my picture in the paper − just a little one − with every article I write. I don't need to dress up and spend thousands to get *my* picture taken.' It was cruel but effective. He could see a hurt, misunderstood look spreading across Karen's face. She usually assumed that look just before he succeeded in reducing her to tears.

'But a girl's wedding's the greatest day of her life. Everybody says so. I'm not uneducated, anyway. I've got four CSEs and I spent a year on day release, learning about making wreaths and business management. I won the Best Floral Tribute section in my class that year. That bowl on the mantelpiece was what I won and a voucher for Stoner's — the undertaker's on Lavender Hill that also sells furniture. We could get something together if you like. We could put it towards a new bed head. I like those padded ones, don't you? I like the bowl best, though — it's lovely — cut glass, you know.'

Nigel meditated on whether smashing her trophy might be the best way to make a clean break. He lacked Gina's panache for throwing things. He had been brought up with a lot of fine furniture and had always been conscious of its value. Kicking the Sheraton cabinet quietly had been as far as he had ever gone in destructiveness. (His parents had never even noticed the faint scratches. They had a French polisher in occasionally to deal with things like that.) Perhaps he could bring himself to back into Karen's bowl? On the other hand, if it was accidental she might even forgive him. He opted for smashing her china dog instead. It was obviously very cheap, so she wouldn't expect compensation. He hated its silly expression. A past boyfriend had brought it back from a holiday near Genoa. It had horrible china curls all over its head like a lousy perm and a red-silk bow round its throat. The rest of the body was yellow. It made nodding dogs seem in good taste.

'Why don't you give that piece of rubbish to Oxfam?' he said, picking it off the mantelpiece roughly.

'But it's got sentimental value, as they say. In any case, Darren might notice if he came round.'

'He won't come round,' Nigel said maliciously. 'Didn't you say he had a wife and a couple of kids now and worked in Basingstoke? Oh no, he won't come round. He's got shut of you. He wouldn't be stupid enough to come back.' He could see that Karen was pondering whether to let one of her tears fall. She cried fairly easily and it usually had some kind of effect. He thought she would probably hold them back this time, as she had mascara on. Black tears generally lose all sympathy.

Karen decided to arouse his jealousy instead. 'I've got plenty of other boyfriends, you know,' she said. 'And they're not old like you.'

Nigel was stunned. He'd never seen himself as old. He wasn't really old, he reasoned – the mid-thirties weren't even middle-aged. Men were different – thirty-six was only old for a woman. He had kept his shape. 'At least I'm *old* enough to know better than to buy a crappy kitsch china schweinhund like this,' he retorted. He knew she wasn't up enough in foreign words to understand him. He suspected she would think that kitsch was something you ate in a wine bar. Karen watched in puzzled amazement as he dropped the thing into the wastepaper basket. Its long neck hit the metal rim and the head was severed. Nigel thought it looked very much like that of a French aristocrat, with all those curls. It rolled bumpily under the bed. Karen bustled round with a pan looking for pieces.

'There might be bits in the luxury pile,' she said.

'What do you think of me now?' Nigel retorted. He was terribly disappointed she hadn't flown at him or reacted more strongly. He hated women who bustled around doing housework. He always wanted to be the most important thing in the room.

'Well, I won't cry over spilt milk,' Karen said as she finally recovered the last smithereen of dog. 'But I think you ought to see a psychiatrist. I think you're having what they call a nervous breakdown. I'll come and see you in the mental hospital if you promise not to cause a scene. I might bring you some flowers, even.'

'Oh, yes, second-hand ones you'd resuscitated with bleach, you mean bitch!'

Nigel was shown out with Karen muttering 'Well!' behind him. He realized, then, that a little professional criticism was all that was needed to finish their relationship. It usually does the trick with anyone who loves their job. He reckoned he had done her a service, smashing her dog. Her place looked in better taste already. If only he'd been able to finish off the plastic swan and the weeping-kid picture there'd have been some hope for the flat. He wondered if he'd have made a good interior designer. He imagined himself in people's homes, earning money by displaying his natural taste. Then he remembered the one designer he'd met — gay — and had second thoughts. Besides, Carl had told him that it was a terrible job for a man of taste. He had complained of having to include people's disgusting favourite items — the photographs on kidney-shaped dressing tables, the vile pictures and ornaments. The only way to design tastefully was to start from scratch, he had said.

16

NUISANCES AS ISOBEL AND KAREN HAD BEEN, NIGEL FELT DEPRIVED at being left with only his wife. There were times when he suspected he was just a meal ticket to her. After all, she had not given up any of her friends for him. The only answer was to find himself someone new. He could tell that several of his students at Kent fancied him. He was certainly the most personable lecturer there. All the other lecturers were at least as married as he was and he, at any rate, had all his hair.

Nigel's novel was not doing quite as well as he had hoped. It had sold a respectable few thousand – mostly to the literary and those who hoped to be part of that world. Being an occasional reviewer himself he was praised by other reviewers who were also creative writers on the old 'you scratch me' principle. But his book did not win any prizes.

Writing, Nigel had always felt, was quite a woman-pulling profession. It definitely had more charisma to it than the Civil Service or teaching. Nigel was proud of his reviews and would have liked another woman to show them to. Gina had never had the slightest bit of interest in his writing. Whenever he mentioned his novel she told him that only *her* work was 'true art'. 'The artist', she said, 'is never accepted in her time.' Nigel had slight doubts as to what her work actually was. He didn't think she threw knives these days and mercifully she hadn't sung 'The Cowboys' Christmas Party' since their time in Chelsea. Occasionally he came in on her while she was engaged in odd projects – dressing up and prancing round their small bedroom, or reciting. Sometimes she had an audience, sometimes not. Sometimes she was directing others while someone held a

Super-8 camera. One day he found her being rolled across canvas by two women in overalls. She was naked except for a tampax and a lot of acrylic paint. She sprawled awkwardly as one of the women lost control of her legs. Nigel remembered he had never liked her body. He rarely saw her naked, which was a relief to him. He had once summed her up to a female student, after several lagers, as 'no tits to speak of and even less bum'. Gina usually wore old dresses and woollies when in bed with him and always locked the bathroom door tightly when she took a bath. He looked at the canvas, trying to track out the familiar hated form. The print of her body was vague and abstract like those blots psychologists want people to interpret, only this one was cabbage green. There was a central mark somewhere in the splurge that might have been the impression of a nipple, but he couldn't be sure. Gina's friends told him that this was a 'personal canvas' and that it had more integrity than conventional beautified portraiture. Gina forced him to staple it to the living-room wall behind the settee and opposite the television. A lot of her friends dropped by to see it.

Occasionally, in the interim period while he was still unattached on the side, he talked of consolidating his marriage. It was a good subject, he found, when he was chatting up his students. He liked to hint that his relationship with Gina was some sort of *grande passion* and that she was the love of his life. One or two of the girls were impressed and imagined some dark, passionate, beautiful, Sophia-Loren type lurking in the background. He had said that he was 'married with one son' on his book jacket, too, as if it was some unusual career. In a way, it was. It took a lot of effort and explanations. It had something of the quality of a full-time job — a rather unpleasant one. Nigel also told every journalist proudly that he was 'married with one son', although he made damn sure they didn't interview him at home, where they might meet his wife, or worse still, her friends.

Anthony stayed happily normal through everything. Gina

had wanted him sent away to school. She had never liked looking after him. Nigel dared to disagree with her – he had hated his own school and he thought he divined Gina's reason for wanting Anthony out of the way. Perhaps she felt she might look old with a gangling adolescent son round the place. After they had quarrelled, Gina lurked at a bend of the stairs and trod hard on Nigel's foot as he came up. One of his toes was broken as a result. He didn't care. He just limped around gaining more sympathy from his students by hinting what a brute his wife was.

Nigel wanted a male ally at home in the shape of Anthony. It made him feel less vulnerable. Anthony sometimes dared to do the things that Nigel only thought of. He could be encouraged into drawing moustaches on the profiles on the curtains or adding to the green nude in the living room. Anthony could be quite inventive. He even forged a plan for growing cress pubic hair at a point in the canvas. They both spent a little time concealing a wad of wet blotting paper and seeds, then cutting small nicks for the cress to grow out of. Anthony tended the canvas for weeks, watering the relevant spot discreetly with a sponge. The paint surface grew a little cracked and mouldy, but nothing else seemed to be happening. Eventually Anthony took the pad away and found a few albino strands growing behind. He replaced the pad and teased these out through the slits. Gina remained in blissful ignorance, while Anthony reduced his father to a state of helpless laughter every lunch time by demanding egg-and-cress sandwiches.

'We have no cress,' Gina would storm. 'You are old enough to get your own food, like your fool of a father.'

Nigel sometimes saw that he was a fool to have put up with everything. It was not something that he could admit to the outside world, though. Better to go on as before than do that. He told various stories when journalists interviewed him about the book and pryed into his background. Sometimes he talked of marrying Gina in the sixties to give her citizenship. She was a 'stateless person', he pretended, one of the children of the war. It seemed more romantic than the truth. However, Nigel enjoyed whingeing more than lying. He saved all his problems up for sympathetic women who were not about to write a piece on him. He liked to keep the story of his life ambiguous. The substance of one interview always conflicted with the next. People got tired of interviewing him because they felt they were being made fools of.

Nigel went on for years basking in the glory of his first book. He made jibes at the expense of more energetic writers, saying that they were cheap and did not rewrite enough. He decided to go for the label of being a careful writer. He could get more literary respect that way. If he produced a book about once every five years, he could pretend to have been working on it all that time, even if he had cobbled it together only in the last two or three months.

Anthony was now away at the university where his father had taught. Inevitably, he was studying English and Italian. Nigel and Gina were left to each other's tender mercies. There had been no other woman in his life for quite a time.

CHAPTER

17

THE BIG FOUR-0 GAVE NIGEL A BIT OF A JOG. HE WAS OFFICIALLY middle-aged now. But then, what did he have to worry about? Men were 'distinguished' at forty; it was only women who turned into old bags.

He celebrated his birthday by going out and getting drunk. He was bought a few drinks by workmates then took off on his own, round various bars, to finish the job properly. 'I'm gonna be stinking pissed when I get home,' he muttered. 'That'll serve Gina right.'

Four Bacardis, three gins and two lagers later — he'd bought the lagers himself — he was stinking pissed. The barman even told him he'd had enough — something they rarely do unless they think a client's about to throw up over the upholstery or start taking his clothes off. A young tart took charge of Nigel. She was semi-amateur. Trade had been bad that night so she thought he'd be her last trick. She took him back to her Streatham pad by taxi, paying for it out of his wallet. He was too limp to argue. The taxi driver helped him upstairs; he'd been tipped most generously.

In the morning Nigel tried faintly to argue about money. Caroline claimed she'd bathed him, massaged him and that he'd had her several times dressed in school uniform. He wasn't sure which of them was meant to have been in school uniform. He still seemed to be wearing his favourite shirt and jeans. His clothes looked undisturbed, if a little rumpled, apart from a sort of embossing of vomit on the front breast pocket of his blue silk shirt. He rather doubted Caroline's story, but it was flattering that any woman should think she'd had him. Besides, his head ached too much to argue. She had to take all the money in his wallet, she explained, because her 'business manager' would beat her up if she didn't turn in the profits. He would be coming round to collect in a few minutes' time. He was a very big ex-boxing and judo champion, apparently. Perhaps Caroline didn't actually have a business manager, but had found that the mention of one proved effective. Nigel did not risk arguing in case she was telling the truth. He still owed her a fiver more than he had on him, she complained. 'I'll make the cash up for you, though,' she went on. 'You can pay me next time you see me. Maybe I'll give you a discount, too. I always do that for my regular customers.'

The word 'customer' was a turn-off to Nigel. He did not need to pay for it. He was an attractive man. He determined not to give Gina any housekeeping this week to make up for his losses. He cadged fivers off various old school friends and workmates to tide him over until he could get to the bank.

After a week or two's good behaviour Nigel began to feel the need to prove to himself that he could pick up a genuine, bona-fide amateur about the same age as Caroline — someone young enough to be his daughter, in other words. This time he decided to take very little in his wallet. He didn't want anyone mercenary. He would go to a bar late and sip a long drink very slowly. He would sit down next to a woman who already had her own full glass in front of her.

Alison was a travel agent's clerk, although she didn't express it to Nigel like that. She was involved, she said, in fixing up tours for VIPs and high-powered executives. Many of her gentleman clients were foreign and even the odd Arab prince had come to her office. Nigel liked the sound of all that — he thought parts of her story might be an exaggeration — the Arab princes — but he recognized a good PR job when he heard one. He wished that one of the journalists who'd interviewed him had expressed the substance of his life and work in such up-market, romantic terms.

Alison was greatly impressed when she heard Nigel was a writer. She evidently had no concept of books other than best sellers. She wondered if he might be Jeffrey Archer in disguise doing his research. Nigel said 'Your place or mine?' when they'd both duly impressed each other with lies. He had forgotten all about Gina, as he usually did when he chatted up pretty girls. Luckily for him Alison didn't say 'Yours'. Instead, she let him know that she never took guys home on a first date. He liked her Americanese. She let him know also that she was a virgin and wanted to save it for someone special. She was tired of younger men: 'They only think about one thing.' Nigel determined to impress her by his abstinence and sensible qualities. He told her that he respected her. They fixed a date for the weekend and he kissed her goodbye. He was reminded of Karen. Alison had that same sweet naivety and the same hard, pursed mouth. He would have liked something a bit more yielding. He couldn't help being reminded of a cat's tight, shell-pink rectum. But he supposed yielding mouths belonged to fast women who might be more risky.

He slapped on a little of a new musk aftershave that was supposed to make him irresistible — not too much, he hated obviousness in men. He also combed a little Grecian 2000 into his hair for several days before his date with Alison. He was careful not to do too complete a job — that kind of thing was noticeable. He'd often despised older men for hasty, inept dying operations. He left a sprinkling of grey at the sides. He had read an article on Mills and Boon books, which said that young girls liked the distinguished professional older man.

Alison met him in the same bar. Unfortunately, he soon realized, she saw her Pernod as a prelude to an evening somewhere else. Nigel had never thought of a drink like that. He usually drank a half of lager unless someone bought for him. He had perfected the knack of making one really last, for which he was known and hated by several West-End barmen. He wanted to find a woman of Alison's age, but one who'd be content, like the journalist old bags he knew, with one drink and a few quiet complaints about his wife and related problems. He hankered after the cheapness of Isobel and Fran. They were too old for him, though — both well past thirty.

Nigel had once made himself unpopular at the office by writing in his column that women past thirty should shoot themselves. 'In fact,' he'd gone on, 'it would be most convenient if they did it on their birthdays. Without all those old bags the world would be a much prettier place. There would be just young women for men to compete for.'

A host of angry letters from women over thirty who thought themselves beautiful had arrived at the office. He had to write a tiny snippet insisting that it was irony and the editor printed a token letter by a woman who had pointed out that if only young girls were left — and not enough of them to go round — only rich old men would have any chance of sex. 'No woman', she had written, 'genuinely fancies a man old enough to be her father. The mercenary ones simply put up with them and pretend that they love them for what they can get out of them. If the old fool doesn't die soon enough, or they get the chance of a better deal, it usually ends in divorce.'

'Bloody feminist,' Nigel had muttered. He didn't take that copy of the paper home. He didn't want Gina using those arguments next time he told her how much better he could have done for himself.

Apart from the expense of taking Alison to the cinema, Nigel's evening out was all he could have hoped for. He was seen with a pretty young woman, was able to paw her a little without having the effort or commitment of doing more and had also enjoyed himself complaining about his wife. Alison had shown enough respectable horror on discovering that he was married to prove she was a nice girl. He assured her that he was unhappily married, never had sex with his wife though they slept in the same bed, and that they often thought of divorce. (He wasn't really lying — they did often think of it even if they didn't get down to it.) Alison's eyes had brightened at the word 'divorce' and she said that she would go on seeing him.

Nigel got taken home to meet her parents next. He wasn't

entirely happy about that. They lived in a council house in Wembley, which was a little off-putting. They had gnomes in the garden, which was even more off-putting. Alison looked quite like her mother – only the mother was over the top and wore too much make-up. She was definitely an old bag. She told Nigel proudly that Alison could have been anything she wanted, even an air hostess.

On his way home Nigel began to have doubts. Alison was already becoming too much of a fixture in his life.

Nigel went out regularly, picking up girls. If there were enough of them, none of them would dare to pin him down, none of them could claim she was anything special. It proved expensive, though. He still had not mastered the art of picking up a girl half his age who was not after his money, but he had found ways to avoid spending too much. He regularly forgot his wallet and credit cards and got them to pay for him or be content with what could be bought on a little small change. He made great promises for future dates but failed to ring the numbers they gave him. Still, even operating in small change every night was expensive.

He told himself it was all good copy for his next novel. He showed his editor, Jo, a few chapters, but her firm would not offer such a good advance as on the previous book. These affairs, she complained, were even less real than the last lot. Being a mere woman she objected to phrases like 'twinkling nipples'. 'Nipples don't twinkle – you must have fallen asleep looking at the fairy lights on the Christmas tree,' she scoffed. 'Why don't you include some women who can talk sensibly – some who've heard of feminism and can spell it? All the pick-ups you've mentioned are daft as a brush. They're not even colourful, Dickensian daft. Insipid daft doesn't make good copy. You're definitely not the thinking woman's crumpet, are you?'

He was tempted to tell her to hire someone from the gutter press if she wanted more earthy writing, or some bloody feminist if she wanted a sensitive novel. He turned red up his right side while she was speaking. He found that only his right side could react. It was a strange physical peculiarity of his.

He continued with the book in a half-hearted way. Early criticism makes writing difficult. If only he'd finished his new masterpiece before he'd submitted it to her critical eye. The problem was that he needed money. Maybe someone else would like the look of these few chapters. A male editor might better appreciate the merits of his style: 'twinkling nipples' was the kind of phrase that would appeal to a real man. What did Jo know?

Nigel began to think of other ways to finance his 'research', since a large advance was not forthcoming. He stopped giving Gina housekeeping. He usually ate out – there was rarely any food in the house. Gina was anorexically thin, more through meanness than design; she only ate when other people provided. Her diet was mostly handfuls of peanuts and crisps from private views she had attended. She had several artist friends who invited her and it was easy enough to crash into other ones if you knew when and where. People rarely asked for your invitation card. She used to cycle to them to save money. She had taken over Nigel's old bike. (He had always used a lady's bike as a teenager because he thought the middle bar on a man's one might do him a mischief if he cocked his leg over it carelessly.) Once inside a gallery, Gina would sidle up to the bowls and shovel large handfuls of nuts or crisps into the pockets of the loose Chinese quilted jacket that she usually wore. (In the first few, more romantic months after her return she had shared these with Nigel.) Occasionally there were canapés, too. She preferred to eat as many of these as she could on the spot, as they were too messy to take away. Afterwards she'd have a glass or two of wine to wash it all down. She liked to save any money she got off Nigel and had her own private account in a building society the other side of London. She didn't spend the money on clothes – he suspected she just liked to see it mounting up as an escape fund. Nigel had found the pass book, but Gina tore it from his hands before he could see how much was in her account. He was used to her going through his pockets while he was asleep and taking what she could. He made sure that he never had much on him. He didn't like to risk her rage by challenging her directly. Other men's wives did proper jobs once the children were off their hands. He sometimes wondered why she hadn't thought of that. Yet, poorer as it made him, he took a certain pride in keeping his wife. He could pretend she was a good housewife, cook and mother to other men who were disgruntled at their wives' brilliant careers.

Not giving Gina housekeeping didn't seem to solve Nigel's financial problems. He had never given her a vast amount, anyway. It had been the same sum for years. Gina got nastier and nastier when she didn't have money; she hit him much more than before.

'You are no good to me,' she used to say. 'You do not give me things like other men and you cannot do sex.' Her English was still slightly odd.

'I don't want to,' Nigel would retort. 'You're too old for sex at forty, or is it forty-one?' (He had always had difficulty remembering exactly when her birthday or any other girl's was.)

The interchange would usually end with Gina kicking Nigel on the shin, clawing him or hitting him if she had something in her hands. Sometimes she would stay away for a day or two. He never knew quite where she went. When she came back she would say, 'You think I am too old for sex, eh?' He was so convinced that she was, he just assumed she had stayed with some girlfriend to try to make him jealous. He had quite enjoyed that kind of jealousy for the first few months of their marriage. Now, though, he couldn't care tuppence.

Nigel began selling review copies – his own and any others he could cadge – to give a little boost to his income. He had been too lordly to do this at one time, preferring to give them as Christmas presents. While the booksellers were looking at his books he would quietly nick a few of theirs to sell to another shop. It was a good little earner;

it paid the grocery bills for the week – his own, anyway. He had keen eyes and quick hands, so it was a long time before he got caught.

Nigel ran through more and more young girls. The youngest he managed to pull was just seventeen. He was very proud of that. He mentioned it to several of his male colleagues. 'You mind she doesn't shag you to death,' one of them said. 'These young girls wear an old man's heart out. Look at that sports editor over there – he's had four marriages and as many heart attacks. Best way to go, though.' When he heard this, Nigel felt rather funny. He knew he wasn't old, of course, so there was nothing to worry about. Besides, shagging had not come into it. He sometimes had sex with girls when drunk, he believed, but not otherwise. There was a lot to be said for flirtation and mutual admiration. It was more reassuring than anything committed. His young girls didn't really give him erections. He just felt pleased when he thought about the kudos of pulling someone half his age or less.

The curious truth about his erection was that he could never remember having a very full one. As far as his cock was concerned he felt somewhat in the position of a toddler trying to fly a kite. He'd see it raise slightly, but he couldn't quite get it up. Some of his male colleagues boasted about how they'd felt with various women, raising an arm to show what they'd been like. That was all alien and too coarse for Nigel. He couldn't recollect anything similar having happened to him. He reckoned that gentlemen didn't have such experiences. Although he liked to be admired for his prowess, he didn't like male-talk of that kind. He never peed in front of other men. He used to flee into a cubicle at the sound of approaching feet. He had never joined in the masturbation rites at school, either. For a while he had thought that his masturbating friends all had VD and that it was a dollop of pus coming out when they pulled at themselves. He didn't want anything like that to happen to him. Some of his school friends had thought he was a cissie. One or two had tried to see if he was interested in other things, but he wasn't. There were occasions when Nigel had wondered himself whether he was homosexual. He certainly liked men more, but then he liked manly men not 'bloody queers', so he had to be all right. Besides, some of the women Nigel got drunk with told him he'd had sex with them, so he knew he was normal.

CHAPTER

18

THE COARSENESS OF THE MEN AROUND HIM AND THE ANTAGONISM of feminists made Nigel decide to adopt a more cynical pose. While he went on picking up young girls, he talked in a blasé way of lust being 'expense of spirit in a waste of shame'.

'I expect you don't expend much spirit if you're still the old Nigel we all know and love,' Fran said. 'The most you ever bought me was a lager.'

Nigel didn't mind her joke about the spirits. It was quite a good one; he must remember to use it himself. He didn't like her calling him old, though. There was a time when he wouldn't have noticed it, but these days he was a little touchy about things like that, especially as Fran was now living with a man fourteen years younger. He'd thought her a little too old for his own purposes, but always assumed she was there for the taking. He comforted himself by assuming that she was just a mother-figure to the young man and there couldn't possibly be any sex in it.

Nigel knew that he would be the choice of any thinking woman, in spite of Jo's remarks. He hadn't aged much in the last twenty years. The mirror told him he still had his youthful figure, and the grey was all covered now. His supple skin had no lines to speak of; he preserved it with various expensive creams and face masks. He would flirt with the girls who sold them to him and pretend they were a present for his mother. Although he believed thoroughly in the ability of these products to fill out the tiny character lines around the eyes and mouth, and to smooth his neck, he did not want to admit he was buying them for himself. He resented the price of all these things and toyed with the idea of starting a relationship with a beautician with a view to getting free samples. But beauticians might be greedy financially, he reckoned, so that idea was discarded together with that of shoplifting. Beauty counters and salons kept a tight watch, so it would be impossible. He did however manage to shoplift vitamins and minerals galore from his local health store. Zinc, he had been told, did wonders for the older man. They had a few creams, too – aloe-vera gel and wheat-germ oil; these could be used as an alternative to the more expensive big-brand names. He began to despise other men who did not look after themselves. The care he took, as well as his natural good looks, continued to provide him with plenty of pick-ups in his early forties.

One day while he was in his favourite bar, busy impressing a young temp, his wife walked in. He turned away and fiddled with his nails, hoping she wouldn't notice him. The girl asked what the matter was. Then Gina came over to their table. Nigel looked up apprehensively. He wondered if he should make introductions. Would Gina cause a scene? Would she hit him in public as she did at home? Much to his surprise she chatted to him quite amicably for a change. She even said 'Hello!' to the girl. She had not mentioned being married to him, so he didn't mention it either.

'Who's that?' the girl asked.

'Oh, just an old acquaintance,' Nigel answered. He felt that was true in a way.

Nigel's wife often appeared to haunt him after that. He didn't see any reason to mind it, but he wondered how she had developed such a good instinct for discovering his whereabouts. There was a sort of uneasy complaisance in their relationship now. While he talked to a girl, she would sit at the bar and talk to the nearest man. He felt the whole thing was turning into a game in which each watched the other and paralleled their next move. If he went off with one of his girls he felt sure she would find someone to disappear with. He despised her looks now, so he scoffed at the idea that it could be for sex. Presumably she would just go and have a coffee with some old, lonely man. That was about her level. The thing that perturbed him slightly, though, was that most of the men she talked to were young rather than old. In fact they were extremely young. He felt she was stepping out of her class, in a sense. Yet they weren't attractive men; she seemed to have a line in short, greasy misfits. None of them were up to him in looks.

Nigel got cross only when she brought the short, greasy misfits home. His house was his workplace. Gina shouldn't interfere with that. She had never helped with any of the bills, so he felt that the house was his alone. Gina's latest pick-ups were even worse than her circus friends.

Nigel also resented the expense of entertaining. He did it once a year, on Boxing Day. He used to buy in a lot of delicacies to pretend to his family that Gina could cook. The delicatessen was owned by a most enterprising Indian who opened at all the times when other places were shut. It was worth the expense of ready-roasted game and home-made puddings and cakes, Nigel felt, to cover up. Gina didn't agree. She often quarrelled with him after these family occasions and threw the remains of the feast at him. She couldn't bear it if he spent money on anything consumable.

'Your family is not worth this £31.34 you have spent.' (She always found and inspected till receipts from the bottom of his carrier bags.) 'Your family are just English pigs – they eat too much! They have no culture like the Buffons. My great-grandmother was from Paris.'

'The Paris sewers,' Nigel muttered inaudibly as she cracked the Stilton dish over his head.

The only times Gina brought food in were those when she was entertaining. Nigel would try to find out when, so that he could invite one of his pick-ups as a counterblast. He would provide food for his visitor and Gina did the same for hers. But she'd let him have a slice of the cake she'd brought in if he gave her and her friend fruit or ice cream – whatever he'd bought. Gina often produced a cake from the pocket of her useful jacket. He suspected she'd shoplifted it, as she usually had some small item in a plastic bag, too. He felt she was definitely too mean to spend her own money on entertaining. After all, she even resented him spending his. He theorized that she went into a shop and lashed out a bob or two on something like a tin of baked beans. While she was going round she would collar some dearer item off the shelves, slipping it into one of her capacious pockets. He didn't care as long as she didn't get caught and ask him to pay the fine. He was all in favour of anything that kept their costs down.

Once tea with their guests was over, Gina would put away her cake. He never found where she hid her food. He took to hiding some secret supplies of his own in his desk. She usually found those, though, just as she usually found any cash or letters that he'd hidden from her.

When the food had been safely put away, the symbolism would start. Sometimes she claimed that the wine her friend had brought was 'sweeter than any you have given me'. In winter when she entertained she would send him outside to chop more wood for their open fire. As he staggered back with some misshapen logs, she would hand the bellows to her latest friend and say, 'You blow up my fire. You are better at that than Nigel. You are younger.' He didn't really like the way she called him Nigel — it was as if he was a stranger. Symbolism had been fun in his early days with her, but it was something that had turned very sour in a live-in situation. Occasionally he retaliated with his own efforts about the relative sweetness of something his guest had brought, but he usually said it in an unconvinced, muddled way. The English are too down to earth for successful symbolism. Gina's Italian and French ancestry made it come more naturally.

Sometimes Nigel wondered why he had got married. He didn't seem to have the comforts of other men. Occasionally he dropped hints on this matter to Gina. She told him he was lucky to be married to a 'beautiful, intelligent artiste'. Sometimes he quoted this phrase to others in a dazed sort of way.

NIGEL WAS COASTING THROUGH LIFE CONTENTEDLY ENOUGH. HE HAD found a new publisher and his second novel was out. He still wrote articles and gave workshops. And he still picked up bits of stuff.

The new publishers were giving him a launch party and wanted names for the guest list. Nigel's sympathetic male editor agreed to ask all the good-looking women writers he could think of. 'Won't be a long list, old man,' he said to Nigel and they both laughed.

The do was at the home of one of the female directors of the firm. Nigel didn't approve of her. He thought she had too much power for a woman. The old cow was nearly fifty. He looked around for someone attractive to talk to. One of the guests was a rather fey romantic novelist. She had come dressed in pink, inevitably. She reminded him a little of an older Karen, but he wasn't tempted. After all, apart from being all of thirty-two, she was the wife of one of the editors and no woman was worth getting into trouble for. Two others were journalists he knew already. They were a bit tough and masculine in his opinion. Worse still, both were also in their thirties.

'So where are all these good-looking women you were going to invite?' he asked his editor. Then he saw the newcomer. She looked young enough in her skintight, royal-blue jersey dress. Figures like that don't come on oldies, Nigel thought. He cut in on a man who was starting to chat her up – someone who had once given him a bad review. 'Have you got a cigarette?' he asked.

Eleanor, it turned out, was a writer too. She had some modest successes behind her with short stories. He vaguely remembered her name from the literary magazines, where she was quite well thought of. He got a little tired of her complaints that male chauvinism had stopped her getting a book out. He agreed with it all, of course, to ingratiate himself, looking deep into her large, green eyes all the while. He could feel a slight erection coming on – the sort he had in bars when he met good-time girls. He was a little surprised. He thought he had programmed his body not to go for intellectual types – that is, if any woman could be described as intellectual. He went to pee to compose himself. When he came back, Eleanor had gone, so he wasn't able to get her phone number. He thought he'd like to see her again as long as she didn't whinge too much about sexism. She'd be good to be seen with and she had a sense of humour. Looks, youth and professional success – she'd be perfect for upsetting Gina. His wife, much as she might boast of the intellect of her pick-ups, couldn't pretend they were pleasing to the eye. Compared to them, Eleanor had everything.

Nigel could be quite persistent when he had thought of something to make Gina miserable. He wrote to Eleanor. He got her address from his editor, who handed it to him with a nudge and a wink. 'Sounds like a bit of a raver from her stories,' he said. Nigel sent her a nice little note inviting her for a drink. Eleanor wrote back wittily and they struck up a friendship. Eleanor had just been photographed for one of the supplements and it pleased him to be seen with someone in the news.

He was very honest with her about his wife. He told her he was married at once. He also told her in great detail what kind of a woman Gina was. By the second meeting Eleanor knew that Gina's friends walked into their bedroom. By the third she knew how knocked around he was. By the fourth she had heard that Gina was frigid.

Eleanor wasn't a particularly moral type. By the time she's thirty – and Eleanor was thirty in spite of appearances – a woman has usually picked up her share of married men. Nigel's wife was obviously such a monster, too, that it had to be any good woman's Christian duty to save him from a fate worse than death, or at the very least to give him a little light relief. Nigel seemed willing on the surface to receive this. He kept asking her to ring whenever she was in London – she lived in Brighton – so that they could get together. Yet he showed a certain reluctance to touch her, just giving her a few social kisses, one or two, on meeting or parting. Sometimes he forgot and gave them again, which she took to be a good sign.

They got on remarkably well as friends. They shared the same sense of humour as long as they kept off delicate subjects like sexism. Nigel gave her a little useful advice on publishers too. When they were not meeting they wrote long letters. They wrote freely as if they had known each other for years. Eleanor felt they were the funniest letters she'd ever written; Nigel brought out the best in her writing. She had never found any friend before who liked exactly the same jokes about sexuality and the same bitchings about other writers. With every letter she tried to top her last efforts and woo him with wit.

Nigel sensed all this and basked in it. As long as she didn't get too serious it was all right. He knew he was good-looking and ought to be admired. For the time being she was useful to annoy Gina, but if she got too possessive he would have to drop her. He liked her to phone him for two reasons – it kept his phone bills down and if Gina answered it proved that he was fancied. Gina used to snarl '*Allo!*' down the phone. She was a little uneasy with the letter H and put it in other words, which was confusing; 'hungry' and 'angry' were often made to sound the same. Sometimes she called Nigel to the phone, sometimes not. Sometimes she said simply that she did not know when he would be back and dropped the phone. Eleanor had discussed this reaction with Nigel, hoping that he'd volunteer to do all the phoning in future, but he just assured her that his marriage was an open one.

A few months on in their friendship Nigel began to be sick of the hints of affection dropped by Eleanor. She had the cheek to think he might come to Brighton to see her.

(Why should he spend the fare?) If he had a reading nearby he might of course be able to use her place and still claim hotel expenses, so it would not pay to fall out. On the other hand, Brighton was near enough to get back to London the same night, so that wasn't really necessary. He invented a serious accident for his wife as an excuse not to see Eleanor for a while. She was most solicitous (scheming bitch!) so he told her that his wife was cured and they went back to the same old routine.

When Eleanor's book of short stories was accepted by a publisher he had suggested, Nigel found that he had mixed feelings. He was pleased in a way that his advice had been proved good, but he didn't like the thought that a woman was catching up with him. Eleanor wrote too fast in his opinion. She looked all set to be a book-a-year person once she had the initial break. He toyed with the idea of creating a little angst in her life to slow her down. A writer should suffer and all that – it would be for her own good in the long run. He started to pick the odd quarrel and cancel dates. Eleanor just abused him thoroughly, which wasn't very womanly in his opinion. Perhaps involving Gina more would add a new dimension. The next time Eleanor rang him he would ask her to tea.

CHAPTER
20

NIGEL BOUGHT SOME CHERRIES AS A ROMANTIC GESTURE. GINA'S French blood would make her appreciate the similarity between the words 'cherry' and 'chérie', even if Eleanor didn't understand. Besides, he fancied some. He was a bit bird-like, a picky eater (especially when he was paying), fast in his movements and very thin in the sort of way that brings out the motherly best in women. He cultivated the image.

Eleanor came wearing a red suit, and he felt so turned on that he forgot to put the water in the teapot. His psyche was telling him not to put something wet and warm in something else for her. He had a kind of inbuilt guilt that saved him from most affairs, but also occasionally made a fool of him. He called to Eleanor to come into the kitchen. He could tell his wife afterwards that another woman had been in there. Maybe she would even smell a whiff of perfume. He wished he could instruct Eleanor to leave a hair grip, but she didn't use any. Perhaps it would be worth buying a few feminine trifles to leave lying around? Why, oh why, wasn't Gina there? He hated it when she was tactful and allowed him space to meet women.

They went back upstairs and he talked dirty to Eleanor. He could never resist doing that with an attractive woman. But he avoided sitting on the sofa next to her although she'd left space. He kept himself diagonally across the room as far away as he could. He made periodic dives at the bowl of cherries poised on a coffee table by the sofa. After twenty minutes, they heard Gina come in noisily, scraping her bike against the paintwork in the hall. (How Nigel hated that habit of hers!) He had a brainwave and called her in and introduced her. She ignored Eleanor completely and wouldn't even say '*Allo*'. To punish her, he ordered her to go downstairs and get Eleanor something to eat. He half hoped she'd bring back a burnt-offering, the way she had so often in their first few months of marriage, when she had deigned to cook for him. He wanted to see what Eleanor would do. He had always had doubts about his own past reactions to Gina's behaviour. Part of him wanted to take lessons from people of more decided character. Gina returned, bearing a decent-looking slice from a Victoria sponge, much to his surprise. Perhaps she was getting civilized in her old age. Eleanor ate it slowly. Perhaps it had even been home-cooked. He couldn't really see without his glasses on.

Then Nigel had the bright idea of taking the two women for a drink at his local. He fancied being seen with two women who were at each other's throats. When he and Eleanor got into the hall, he called up the stairs to Gina but she wouldn't come. 'Perhaps you can bring me something back!' she said sarcastically. Nigel rather admired her talent for symbolism. To turn the knife in the wound, he had mentioned to her the name of a local pub that had refused her singing act. He did not take Eleanor there in the end, though, as there was one that was even nearer and cheaper. He was rather cool with her, since drinking wasn't much fun if he couldn't stir it between the two women. He made an excuse and went home early — there was a review he had to write. He felt deeply disappointed in Eleanor's visit. He had figured from her stories that she had a more passionate temperament and had hoped she'd shout and scream at his wife. It had all been very tame. Now he would have to face Gina's displeasure. He did not bring anything back.

Gina was in one of her moods. In fact she hardly spoke for days. After a weekend of brooding silence and no service, Nigel began to think it had all been worth it. When they eventually spoke it was to quarrel. Gina ripped up one of his articles. Luckily he had photocopied it before he provoked her into doing this. 'Your mistress', she said, 'will not be so happy when she gets home. In fact she is probably ill or dying already.' He felt a bit worried at this and started to question her. It was another day before she'd say, 'You made me bring food for your tart so I poisoned it. I sprinkled a little household cleaner on it.'

'You never use household cleaner!' he said. 'Look at this place. I'd be ashamed to bring my boss here or any influential person from work. You never use household anything!'

'Oh, yes I do – to poison your whores. I am too good to serve food to them. The carton I took from the supermarket said "POISON" in big letters, and "Not to be taken internally", so she will be dead by now. I do not care. You are such a bad man bringing women home for me to cook for that the courts would acquit me.'

Nigel went silent and white. He didn't know whether to believe her or not. But why should she lie? He searched the kitchen and found the household cleaner standing by the tea caddy, a sprinkling of white powder beside it on the formica. He went down there only to make tea or hide something in the fridge. Neither of them ever cleaned up. It could well be true, he decided and went to ring Eleanor. At times like these he wished he had married an Englishwoman.

'Oh, is that you, Nigel?' Eleanor answered. 'What a nice surprise. I've only just got up – I'm not feeling too brilliant. I think I've got gastric flu. I had a terrible time last Friday – your paper sent me proofs to correct the same day so I had to struggle up with them. There were so many mistakes I couldn't do it over the telephone. I was sick three times as I was trying to get ready. I had to wash my hair too, before I went out, I looked such a mess. I felt really faint so I went to the pub at the end of the road where your office is – can't remember its name. Anyway, I fell through the door as they opened up. My voice had nearly gone when I tried to order a brandy. I think they thought they had an alcoholic on their hands.'

'Oh, I am sorry,' Nigel said guiltily. It wouldn't do any

good to tell her the truth — if it was the truth. Perhaps it *was* just gastric flu. There was a nasty strain of it doing the rounds at the moment, and she didn't sound that unwell now. It was probably a mercy that she'd been sick. If his wife had put anything on the cake it would be long gone by now. 'Well, give me a ring when you're up in London, or rather before — when you're better, that is. You must come to tea again. I'll ring you.'

He hadn't meant to say that. It just slipped out. Eleanor's warm, inviting voice had that effect on him. Oh well, if she was unwise enough to come to tea, Gina was unlikely to try the same thing again. In his experience she rarely did anything twice. She was not even reliably cruel. On the plus side, if she saw Eleanor alive and well it might frighten her into some sort of submission. People who could live through poisonings, like Rasputin, had to be respected for their vital force.

Nigel decided to leave things a few weeks then issue an invitation to dinner. Dinner would annoy Gina even more than tea. He had often had tea with girls from his workshop. She was used to that. He couldn't fathom why she'd taken such exception to Eleanor. He had never invited anyone to dinner at the house, for the simple reason that they never had anything he could honestly call dinner. When he rang Eleanor he would explain that it was only to be a simple snack. If the worst came to the worst he could cook it himself. He was a mean hand at fry-ups; he'd learnt that at his public school. There were electric rings in most of the studies, and the official meals were somewhat Spartan and not to every boy's taste. With a bit of luck Eleanor might lend a hand. His fried eggs were a bit scrappy: they needed a woman's touch. Sausages, however, he could do to a turn. If he added a bottle of wine, the occasion would be quite festive. He wondered whether to call the invitation dinner or supper. Supper was becoming a fashionable word and could cover a snacky situation better. On the other hand, supper sounded too close to bedtime for his liking. It would be easier to get rid of Eleanor after dinner.

Nigel hadn't heard from Eleanor for several weeks. He felt sure he'd have been told of it at literary do's if she was really ill. Although she wasn't popular with most literary men, they talked about her a lot. It was often said that her new-found reputation was a bubble that would burst once people realized it was just the raunchiness of her work that got her a wide readership. Nigel was inclined to agree. After all, women can't write good classical prose. That, like poetry, his friends said, has always been the prerogative of men.

Eventually, Eleanor rang. Nigel was glad as it saved him breaking his own rules about using the phone. He liked never to call from home; that way he could check up on Gina. He used to pop out and use a pay phone, ringing publishers at awkward times like lunch time so that they had to ring him back. If he knew that none of the call charges on his bill were his, it proved just how often Gina phoned her friends, in spite of any pretences she might make. He could reproach her with it. In the holidays, Anthony sometimes used the phone, of course, but he wasn't there much now. He seemed to prefer to go travelling with his fellow students. He should have finished at university long ago, but he kept taking extra courses, changing subjects and things. Nigel had lost track of it all.

To his surprise, Eleanor was not bowled over by the dinner invitation. She had the cheek to say that she felt his wife wouldn't like it. 'She wouldn't speak to me last time I was in your home,' she complained. Evidently she hadn't suspected anything else.

'You've got it all wrong,' he said. 'She's just gauche.'

'Gauche at forty-five?' Eleanor laughed.

'Well, her English isn't any good.'

'Oh, I suppose I wouldn't be too polite in Italian,' Eleanor gave in graciously. 'I do feel she doesn't want me there, though.'

'I don't even know whether she'll be there,' Nigel went on. 'She doesn't tell me what she's doing. Anyway, if she does turn up, you can tell her to bugger off for all I care!'

Nigel felt very brave shooting his old bugger-off line. He rather hoped that Eleanor would say this, even though other girls hadn't. She might be the only one brave enough. She would do it if she really cared for him, he believed.

Eleanor accepted the invitation in the end, but opted to come to tea. Nigel was looking forward to the occasion and Gina had promised to be especially nice and polite as long as she could have one of her friends there to make up a foursome.

CHAPTER 1

GINA WAS INDEED PERFECTLY NICE AND POLITE WHEN ELEANOR came to tea. Disappointingly so, from Nigel's point of view. This time, Eleanor had brought a cake of her own — she was good at making them. It was an odd gesture, but one he appreciated. He would have preferred a showdown with Gina, but it was fun to watch Eleanor fighting her by stealth. He wondered, as he enjoyed a slice of cherry cake, if he would be able to exploit Eleanor into further baking.

This time, Gina's 'small, greasy artist friend' annoyed Nigel to the point that he had to take Eleanor into his study to talk about them. They weren't doing anything — they were just being polite — but Nigel was slightly afraid that the artist was trying to get off with Eleanor. He had shown interest in her work and talked as if he took it seriously. That was something men rarely did to women unless they had an ulterior motive, Nigel believed. In the end he preferred to leave the man alone with his wife rather than risk losing his latest conquest to him.

They chatted about the artist. Nigel was relieved to hear Eleanor run him down even more than he had. Just to make certain she believed the man was having an affair with his wife, he assured her that, despite his penchant for painting boys, the artist wasn't gay.

Gina and Michel, the artist, had gone off together to some exhibition by the time Eleanor left. Nigel accompanied her, as he was on his way to see his mother. She was throwing a party and had invited him but, as usual, not his wife. She was still trying to get him off with a nice society type. He quite enjoyed the process although he never fancied the women concerned. His mother would introduce him as 'my darling son, Nigel – he's such a talented writer, you know, and his marriage is on the rocks, poor dear!' His marriage had been officially 'on the rocks' for nearly twenty-three years. Sadly, the old bitches his mother lined up were only a few years younger than him. He had once questioned her on this point, saying that a man of his age preferred younger women to be seen out with. She was offended and took it all personally. 'Young girls who go out with men your age are just gold-diggers! When do you ever see a poor man with someone twenty years younger?'

'I'm not rich!'

'Yes, and you don't have anyone twenty years younger.'

'I've had a good few of them, Mummy.'

'Yes, but they pissed off once they found out what your bank balance was, I'll be bound.'

Nigel thought his mother was rather crude as well as not versed in the ways of the world and in what men want. Maybe he would show Eleanor to her as a sample of the younger woman who was not a gold-digger. Eleanor could be presented to his mother, even if Karen and Caroline and all the others couldn't. She wasn't really young enough, though. She was a mere twelve years his junior. He needed some nice girl of Anthony's age to prove his point. He broached the idea of bringing Anthony to his mother's next party, hinting his son needed help in getting a girlfriend, too. 'You get some of your friends to bring their young daughters,' he said to his mother. 'Doesn't matter if they're still at school, as long as they're over the age of consent and on the Pill. I don't want him getting into a mess.'

Nigel had often thought of stealing a girlfriend off his son, but didn't have quite the same tastes. Unfortunately Anthony usually chose college friends and Nigel didn't really take to bluestocking women. Eleanor was a bit of a trial to him at times. He preferred the sort of woman who put her foot in it with grammar and things; that way he could feel superior by correcting her at the time and having a laugh at her expense later with his male colleagues.

He speculated on the bevy of beauties his mother would

line up next time. Perhaps he could arrange for Anthony to go sick at the last minute. The more he thought about schoolgirls, the more distasteful became the forty-year-old debs that his mother had lined up for him. He still turned on the charm, however. It was all practice, after all. He was able to do a good impression of a struggling young writer, as he looked more late thirties than early forties. He had been careful with his hair. As the women talked and asked stupid questions about his novels he imagined putting them in the next one. It would be nice to be totally irresponsible, he felt, and get so stinking drunk that he could say what he liked to them. As he shook hands and tolerated all the small-talk, he thought of saying, I don't think much of you, you old trout. You've got jowls. Just because you've bleached your moustache, don't think it doesn't show. If you've got a daughter half your age I'd rather screw her instead. He dared himself to say it to each new person. By the time he got to the oldest, a tiresome socialite friend of his mother's, he started: 'I don't think much. . . .' His voice quavered as he heard the silence around him. He looked at them all and knew he couldn't. 'I don't think much of T.S. Eliot,' he faltered.

That would have made an impression at a literary party, but the old trout just replied, 'Silly boy, I don't think you've been listening to a word I said!'

Nigel got back to an empty house with no Gina. She was still off with Michel, presumably, trying to make him jealous. He wasn't. He was pretty sure that Michel was gay, whatever he had said to Eleanor. And his wife was definitely frigid and old. She wouldn't enjoy sex with another man when she had never enjoyed it with him. After all, he was better-looking than any man he had ever come across. He took more care of himself and he had great natural style. She was damn lucky to have pulled him as a husband. And Eleanor was damn lucky to have him as an escort once in a blue moon. They didn't know how lucky they were. And there were all the other women he'd made lucky too – all the hairdressers he'd flirted with, all the travel agents, florists and girls in bars. They had all been lucky to be seen out with him. When he was a famous, rich, literary-establishment figure living in Antibes or somewhere they would all realize it.

CHAPTER
22

IT WAS THE SUMMER HOLIDAYS AND ANTHONY HAD COME HOME FOR good, or rather until he found a job. The house felt over-crowded and lacking in privacy with him there. It was big enough for two but not really for three, especially when one of them was a great big lout. Anthony was always on the phone, rushing about like a bull in a china shop, or lying in bed till twelve with one or other of his girl-friends.

Nigel liked to lecture Anthony occasionally about getting girls into trouble. It made him feel superior and worldly wise. He liked to quote other men on the subject too. 'My headmaster always used to say: "Never sleep with a woman unless you're prepared to marry her!"'

'Your headmaster was gay, wasn't he? Anyway, you can bloody talk. Mum got you into trouble all right with me, didn't she? That's what you've often said. Maybe you're not my dad, even. I think of you as my father, of course, when it comes to Christmas presents and topping up my grant, but I'm not sure you've got a blood right to lecture me.'

'All I mean is, you should be a bit more careful,' Nigel said primly. He didn't appreciate slurs on his manhood – even jokey ones. If Anthony was somebody else's he could at least have the decency to shut up about it like his mother had.

'Oh, you think I should have a kept woman like Ma – not very modern, that. I'm young and beautiful, *I* ought to be kept if anybody. I expect I could get some nice older woman to do just that. Perhaps I'll learn to drive and be some film star's chauffeur.'

Nigel looked at his son. No, he wasn't beautiful – his skin was burnt a little pink and his elbows and feet were too big.

Although not unattractive, he was cut in a rougher mould than his father. He lacked his elegance and finesse. Nigel wondered if any film star would be discerning enough to employ *him* if *he* applied for a chauffeur's job. He reckoned he'd fit much better into Hollywood and high society. He had had a gentleman's upbringing. The local grammar school had put too much of a gawky human edge on his son's image. The thing that worried Nigel most about his son's affairs was that they made him feel randy. He wanted to have a succession of girls to show off, too. As it was, he just sat in the room below, hearing those sounds and trying to write. Everything he wrote on those days seemed prurient. There were even more twinkling nipples per square inch of prose. He would have liked to have a girl of his own in there, instead of all the dull books to review, and the first scribblings of the rough draft of his new novel. It would have been nice to have had somebody so that they could have been turned on together by the faint giggles and murmured conversation coming from upstairs. Gina was not turned on by these sounds. She used to get angry and go and pull the bedclothes off Anthony and his friends to make them get up and get out. She screamed and swore at them. She was especially angry if the girls dared to eat any of her food or drink her coffee. She even hid the toilet paper so that guests could not use any.

Nigel asked Eleanor round once more and they were left on their own for a while. He played soft romantic music, hinted about the goings-on upstairs, which had temporarily gone silent, and gazed into her eyes. His wife was lurking in the basement all the time Eleanor was there, so that he did not feel safe getting close. Otherwise, he told himself, he would have suggested a dance and gradually manoeuvred her closer to him until nature took its course. He liked the phrase 'nature took its course' – he often used it in his novels. He didn't like actual descriptions of penetration. He used his best prose on the earlier stuff about tongues meeting and breasts being cupped.

He had a laugh after Eleanor had gone. 'The poor cow's

brought me another cake,' he said to Gina. 'She really must be smitten.'

'Perhaps she was only trying not to get poisoned,' Gina said. They giggled and poked fun at Eleanor as they ate piece after piece of the cake. 'We would never 'ave to buy food for ourselves if I half-poisoned all your stupid little fans,' she said. 'Not that she is little. She has a big bottom.'

Nigel felt they were close for a few moments before the customary iciness set in. He enjoyed the brief flash of jealousy and the home comforts. Eleanor *was* just a stupid fan, of course. His wife was often right in her perceptions of people. Even if she wasn't attractive or sexy, Gina had some uses as a friend and confidante. He always told her about his affairs. He valued advice because he found it almost impossible to make decisions. Or rather, he could *make* them, but just didn't feel like abiding by them a few hours later.

'Eleanor', Gina had said, 'is not an equal. She isn't a fellow professional − a woman can't be. You told me so.' Eleanor wasn't much of a woman, either; Gina had pointed that out to him, too. If she had been, she would have married and had babies by now. What a lucky escape! He had nearly saddled himself with a desperate, thirty-one-year-old fan. He deserved better than that.

Eleanor rang him a few days later and he was remarkably cool. He toyed with the idea of telling her she wasn't woman enough for him, but decided not to. After all, she was all right to flirt with at parties and escort him occasionally. All the other literary women he knew were old bags of whom he would be bitterly ashamed. He would keep Eleanor on tap for these occasions by writing the odd letter and by making the odd phone call too, when he could quietly use an office phone. He would drop her, of course, sooner or later − or rather, he would engineer it so that she dropped him. That was the gentlemanly way. Gentlemen don't jilt ladies. They just behave like absolute pricks so that the ladies have no choice but to drop them if they have any self-respect.

Nigel's usual way of putting women off had always been to cancel dates with ineffectual excuses. He'd say that he'd suddenly remembered he had to go to the theatre with his family, or to a friend's engagement party. He tried both of these old tricks on Eleanor and got thoroughly told off. She had the cheek to say he ought to cancel meetings only because of ill-health or for work opportunities, not because he'd decided to go out with someone else. If she'd been more of a woman, he believed, she would have meekly accepted his word and left it at that. Others had. She even hinted that he had been bullied into it by his wife. He had told her that he had to be quick on the phone because his literary editor was listening to him. It was the truth, but in the sarcastic letter that followed Eleanor put 'literary editor' in inverted commas. Presumably she thought he was phoning from home — something he'd never do. She seemed to be washing her hands of him. It was what Nigel wanted in theory, but in practice he couldn't bear the whole thing ending acrimoniously, especially with her getting the last word. She'd probably have the bad taste to put him in one of her cynical, satirical stories. Perhaps she wouldn't get another book published if she had enough bad reviews, he hoped. They had been very mixed so far.

When they met at parties Nigel continued to keep up a surface friendship. There was no doubt that he was drawn to her; he would greet her before anyone else in the room, and kiss her, sometimes once, sometimes twice, sometimes cupping her face in his hands. But afterwards his conversation was distant. He often asked if she was leaving. 'I suppose you've got to catch a train back to Brighton now?' he'd say hopefully. The fact was that talking to her either in person or on the phone gave him a sort of erection. It wasn't a full one, but it was enough to give him a little pain. Erections had always done that to him. He never saw sex as a relief to this pain. He usually sneaked off to the lavatory and relieved himself by peeing and thinking of funerals. Masturbation only seemed to make things worse. He had found in school that he didn't seem to have the knack of making himself come. He got more and more tense as he pulled at himself. It was partly guilt and partly a fear that he would not succeed. He could feel his shoulder blades sticking out and a powerful migraine beginning. He always had to leave off before he came, feeling sure his head would burst otherwise. Neither was sex a relief. He only seemed to have had it when he was drunk; he couldn't remember surges of relief, or anything else, for that matter. All he knew was that he had always woken up with a splitting headache afterwards, and often wished he'd had the headache instead the night before.

When he was a child Nigel had thought of peeing as sex. Someone had told him, 'Daddy peed into Mummy on their honeymoon and that was how you were born.' The one pee, he supposed, had been enough to produce three sons at two-yearly intervals. Of course, Nigel had acquired the technical facts at school, but they always felt less true to him. Sex seemed an unnecessary thing in life. You had to pee a few times a day to survive. The other act was like some unsavoury childhood ritual. He sometimes believed that whoever had invented it was insane. Sticking your willy up strange holes had to be riskier than standing over a lavatory basin. There was relief in peeing, that was different. It was nice to fill up with Perrier till your bladder was bursting, then go in the gents and let forth a good stream.

Losing your erection is easy enough if you store up the right anti-erotic thoughts. Nigel secretly wished that there was the equivalent to a girlie mag for men who wanted to be turned off. He felt like starting one for like-minded gentlemen. There must be many thousands of them scattered round Britain. Nigel had a series of personal images – some from his past, some from fantasy. He would remember every time he had been humiliated at school or home, exaggerating the feeling and circumstances involved. If these didn't work it was on to the funerals – huge fantasy ones. He would imagine the dead bodies of some pop stars he had admired, his mother, and a few pets he had owned as a boy. There would be hordes of mourners in very unfashionable black. The bodies would look sordid and ugly, dressed in old, rather soiled nightshirts and laid in open-topped coffins, slightly tilted so that everyone could see the contents. There were piles of bad-taste wreaths around and sickly tremolo organ music. That image almost always worked. It combined several emotions. He'd feel a little bit of pity for his mother and the labrador he'd owned at eight, awe at the dead pop stars and disgust at the lack of fashion and the bad music played for the occasion. That usually brought him down to earth. Of late, though, after his meetings with Eleanor, he had had to go on to his third level of fantasy. He sometimes had to disappear to the lavatory several times when they met in a pub or café. He was afraid she might see him sticking out and start taking him for granted or make unwomanly advances. It didn't pay to let a woman know you cared, or rather that your body did.

The third level of fantasy also involved a funeral − his wife's. He would imagine Gina dead. He would see her in the old holey woollies she wore to bed, rather than an old-fashioned nightshirt. He imagined her screwed into some impossible position in her last spasm, her face looking grey and ugly on the pillow. Then he would think of the under-taker forcing that convoluted form into a cheap coffin and the lid being screwed on. Then came the funeral − another bad-taste affair. Nigel found nothing less erotic than bad taste. There would be the same tremolo electric organ, but this time there would be no crowds of mourners − only a straggle of Buffons doing their circus tricks. When they had all left and her father, the grave-digger, had filled up the grave, Nigel would be alone. Then he would stand and pee copiously on the trodden earth. This trick always worked. He would stand in the gents' cubicle and work his way through the fantasy, peeing in synchronization with the finale. He always felt much better after, but he never dared tell the dream to his wife.

CHAPTER
23

NIGEL AND ELEANOR HAD THEIR FIRST SERIOUS QUARREL A FEW months later. Their friendship had straggled on in a passive sort of way; he'd been to see her in Brighton and played the romantic flirt, talking of *Brief Encounter* in the pub and putting his hand on her knee. He knew he could get away safely because he had a reading back in London that evening, and it couldn't lead to further meetings because he was going away soon. He was taking one or two workshops and creative-writing courses abroad. Then there would be the family holiday to save him. Gina always insisted on one a year, somewhere in Europe – wherever her obnoxious family was performing.

He promised to send Eleanor a postcard, but didn't. He promised to ring when he got back, but didn't. Instead she got in touch with him as he knew she would. She sent him a rather touching little note saying she needed cheering up. Her flat had suffered a lot of damage in the autumn gales and some of her recent writing had been totally destroyed at the first-draft stage.

Nigel rallied round and asked her out for a drink. She would be on her way back from a reading at the weekend and passing through London. She had travelled somewhere way up north – Newcastle or something. He arranged to meet her in his local. It was easiest for him, he explained. Nonetheless, he felt annoyed at Eleanor for trying to wring sympathy out of him in this way. Saturday was an awkward day, too, for a married man. His wife liked to keep track of him then. He couldn't pretend he was delivering articles anywhere.

By the time he met Eleanor he was in a really bad temper. Gina had nagged him and Anthony since they had got up. It was worse in his case, because he was a reasonably early riser. He decided to get shut of Eleanor as quickly as possible. He looked at his watch pointedly as they met.

He did the courteous thing, of course, and asked how her reading had gone. She was full of it. She'd had a really good, receptive, large audience. He hadn't on the one occasion he'd been there – in fact they'd treated him rather badly, although he didn't like to admit as much. They talked a little about his 'troubles back home'. He told her again how cold his wife had always been. Eleanor started hinting at an affair. She had done that before. Nigel liked to be loved and admired; he believed he deserved that, but he resented her thinking that she – a thirty-one-year-old – could pull anyone of his calibre. He changed the subject sharply back to home troubles of another kind. There was no peace there now, he said. Anthony had just left university and was hanging round, not trying very hard for a job. It was disrupting his own writing.

'Oh, you mustn't let anything spoil that,' Eleanor said. Nigel enjoyed her admiration of his writing.

'I'm sorry to have to say that Anthony is turning into an absolute bastard. He treats women like rubbish,' he went on, feeling envious of the quantities of them his son seemed able to pull.

'Oh, most men are shits,' Eleanor said. Perhaps she was meaning to be sympathetic. Perhaps she rather hoped he would say, 'I'm not a shit, am I?' and hold her hand. Her right hand was lying casually on the table. He liked her hands. They were slim, pale and elegant, and she wore colourless or pearl nail varnish. There was nothing vulgar about these hands, not like his wife's plebeian paws with their chilblains and chipped red enamel. He toyed with the idea of holding Eleanor's hand and getting romantic. Instead he used her remark as the perfect occasion for a quarrel. He remembered Gina's summing-up of Eleanor's character and told her that she only saw people as shits because she wasn't woman enough to hold a man. The phrase had rather a stylish ring to it, he'd decided.

Eleanor immediately pointed out that he hadn't exactly held his wife, who was thoroughly unfaithful if half the tales he'd told were true.

'She can't be,' Nigel said. 'You've got it all wrong. She's frigid. There's never been much between us in that way. Besides, she's too old for it at forty-five. We're just good friends.'

'Friends!' Eleanor laughed sarcastically. 'By your own admission she's knocked you around and treated you badly. I wouldn't wish a friend like that on my worst enemy. You don't even look like friends when you're together. Ordinary couples get to resemble each other. You seem like strangers when you meet. You talk as if you haven't seen each other for months, can't stand each other and can't wait to get away.'

In his heart, Nigel knew there was some truth in what she was saying. He did always want to get away when he was with Gina. On the other hand, he realized that if he did, there would be financial penalties. He was also cynical enough to believe that any other woman might be as unpleasant to live with. Better the devil you know.... Eleanor wouldn't be much better than Gina – she was nearly as rude as his wife. When she was talking about Gina's marital infidelities she had called her 'your old French stick'. 'She's not French, she's Italian – well, mostly,' he'd replied piously.

The conversation went from bad to worse. Nigel told Eleanor that he despised her for making a pass at him. He really was shocked at her. Women were not supposed to do things like that. They should always leave it up to the man. He might have made a pass given time. Or he might not. Eleanor was nearly twice the age he felt he deserved, and it had been his ambition for a long time to have a girl just at the point when it became legal. He would do all the foreplay while she was fifteen, then celebrate her sixteenth birthday – to the hour – in style. But he didn't want a virgin as such — they frightened him. He wanted somebody else to have done the persuasion and taught her a thing or two first. Much as he admired schoolgirls, flouting the law was too much of a risk for someone with a public image.

The sixteenth-birthday fantasy was a cherished one, but he hadn't found any takers yet. After a particularly good dinner he had once dreamt that Eleanor had a younger sister of that age. She had turned into Eleanor, in fact. They were doing it in a large double bed in the middle of Westminster Abbey with choir and priests looking on. That was the only real wet dream he could remember having. When he woke up he found a little stain, which he thought must be a map of Ireland, on the sheet. Usually with erotic dreams he woke before the end with a leg half over Gina. The sight of her in the old tatty jumpers she slept in always brought him back to reality. He didn't even have to think about funerals.

Nigel pondered his dream about Eleanor. What did it mean? In the end, he decided that it was more of a metaphysical thing. The centre of Westminster Abbey stood for Poets' Corner. He had fancied being a poet when he was a boy — before he'd been thrust out into the real world to try to earn a living. Eleanor was mainly just a red herring, he decided. The only meaning to that part was that he was on top of — i.e., surpassing — her in public. Still, the dream had felt so real that he couldn't resist ringing her from the office to ask if she had a sixteen-year-old sister he could meet. She had sounded rather puzzled and insulted.

The quarrel was the end of his friendship with Eleanor. She had accused him of leading her on. In his opinion, complaining a little about his wife and talking dirty or romantic by turns did not add up to that. It was normal social behaviour. Eleanor was wrong to try and pretend otherwise. He usually talked and behaved like that with women. It was his way. He couldn't go on seeing her in the circumstances. It was all going to cease to be fun if she wanted any action out of him. By this stage Eleanor was in tears. He muttered 'For Christ's sake!' impatiently and offered her his used hanky. She made do with Kleenex and blotted the black mascara off her face. She still looked attractive, even with black rings round her eyes, he decided. It was rather nice to have a woman crying over him. Still, he had to do the honourable thing. . . . If she couldn't take hints he would tell her he had somebody else. Karen was the one he'd stuck with longest, so he told her about his 'little florist'. 'She has an important job,' he said. 'She makes wreaths and bouquets for VIPs. Embassies sometimes call her.' It sounded better that way. He even told Eleanor her age and name to add credibility. He walked Eleanor to the station in silence and gave her a parting hug. She might think he was a little coarse doing that after saying he despised her, but so what? He fancied doing it. After all, she was the only woman to have cried properly for him.

CHAPTER
24

NIGEL WAS GLAD ON ONE LEVEL TO HAVE SAVED HIMSELF TROUBLE by finishing with Eleanor. He realized soon, though, that there was a problem. He hadn't seen Karen for years. That had been easier to finish. You rarely run into people you know in London; there are too many millions. But he and Eleanor moved in the same set socially. He met her at a literary dinner a couple of weeks later. He half wondered if she'd arranged it; women don't get invited to these things as often as men. They were not sitting next to each other, luckily, but he found himself opposite her accusing face over drinks and remembered the things he'd last said to her. He thought it best to give her a quick kiss and talk as if nothing had happened. He hoped she would be civilized enough not to make a scene.

He could see her lip trembling and hoped she would not cry in public again. He didn't want to be made to look a bastard to his friends. He hoped also that she wouldn't do anything to him. She had rather an athletic body. It seemed possible that she might be into chucking men over her shoulder and spifflicating them. He said 'Hello' nervously. He saw her eyes flicker between his face and his balls. Either it was passionate lust, or she was considering pouring her Perrier full of ice cubes down the front of his trousers. He'd seen that done in a film and had always wondered how it might feel.

The moment passed. Eleanor had obviously decided to drink her Perrier, bite back any reproaches and put a civilized veneer on the occasion. He didn't see her again for quite a while. By the time he did, her new book was out and her publishers had sent him an advance copy. He was on their list of possible reviewers. He read the stories carefully. Rather than carrying the usual disclaimer about the characters bearing no relation to living persons, the introduction said that these were *real* stories from Eleanor's life. Perhaps her publishers had good libel insurance. He was amazed and shocked at the contents of her ten stories. In each one she had an affair with a different man. Why, oh why hadn't she had an affair with him? He recognized the symptoms of jealousy. If only she had been less direct in her approach, he might have managed something. He would have enjoyed the odd weekend in Brighton away from the pressures of London life, if only she'd had a bigger flat. The problem was that she had only one bedroom. If he'd stayed when he went to see her, he would have shown he wanted an affair. He preferred more ambiguity and liked the idea of one or other of them sleepwalking accidentally into the other's room; that would have been less crude than prior agreements. He didn't like women who arranged things. Or if she had come to his place and told Gina to bugger off, obeying his instructions, he might have rewarded her and let her move in with him permanently. The men in Eleanor's stories sounded much cruder than him. They had accepted her situation as it was without these sensitive doubts.

When Nigel went into the *Left Arts Review* he found that a good review of Eleanor's book was ready and waiting. An admirer of hers had written it to ensure some early coverage, having got a proof copy from her publishers. It had to be stopped. Nigel couldn't really review the stories himself – that would look too obvious. But he was temporary books editor while his boss was on holiday, so he could manage to fix something. He handed Eleanor's book to a moralistic old bag he had once done a writing workshop with. He disliked her because she had no sense of humour and was into Rudolf Steiner and spiritualism – she was a trained medium. He had despised her thoroughly ever since she had given him some dire warnings about the state of his aura, and he felt she would be perfect for this review. She was flattered to be asked. She made little money from journalism, having criticized too many auras for her own good. If the literary establishment had thought to compare notes they would have realized that every male aura on and off Fleet Street had come in for a bashing. Nigel gave Margaret Dulally several other books by people he hated as well, while his editor was away, saying that a line or two on each would be enough. The favourable, half-page review of Eleanor's book was scrapped and the two lines by Miss Dulally inserted instead: 'Her prose has all the lyricism of the tabloids. It is a sad document of a young woman's promiscuity in an age when AIDS has made most thinking members of the public chaste.' Nigel laughed maliciously, but hoped that the old medium never got the chance to review his books. What would she think of his twinkling nipples? If he ran into Eleanor he planned to blame the general editor and make soothing noises. She would probably be quite prepared to believe someone else was responsible as she was so besotted with him.

Life without Eleanor was quieter but less fun. He wouldn't have to bear her quips about the unfaithfulness of his wife, but then he didn't have her delightful, amusing letters, either. He missed her physical presence too, and dreamed of her oftener now he did not see her. He thought of patching things up, but felt she would try to force him to an affair in some unwomanly way.

Young girls seemed short on the ground. He believed he was as beautiful as ever when he looked into the glass, but perhaps the AIDS scare had stopped them picking up older men in bars. There didn't seem to be any good-time girls left except, maybe, Eleanor. She seemed a bright, unthinking product of the sixties, intent on enjoying herself when everybody else had settled down. He had asked her about that. She had said, 'Well, I was only a child in the sixties, so I've got to have my sixties now.' If only they hadn't become so friendly, he was sure he would have enjoyed having a relationship with her; but he had a rule about not mixing sex with friendship. That could lead to tiresome complications.

Gina read Eleanor's stories in bed every night for weeks. She was rather a slow reader as English wasn't her first language. After the first two stories she said, 'She is a whore. You had a lucky escape, my Nigel. You must always take my advice. I am a woman of the world. I know a whore when I see one.'

He muttered, 'When you look in the glass.' He altered that to, 'Can you put the light out, dear?' when she bashed him with the book and asked him to repeat what he had said. Life never seemed to change.

CHAPTER

25

NIGEL'S LIFE BECAME AN UNRELIEVED SUCCESSION OF BOOK REVIEWS.
His regular column on the *London Literary Times* had
been axed, but the editor still chucked scraps of work his
way. Other papers did too. He hated reviewing. It was
too much work for too little money, especially when it was
a short review. Editors often cut a vital sentence, too,
and made the whole thing unbalanced. It was a corrupt
world. Often they axed the only approving comments, so
that he looked a complete bastard. Still, he quite liked
making jokes at the expense of other authors. That was
the one consolation. It was nice to home in on the one
naive sentence in a book and quote it, making the author
look like a prat. Nigel made many enemies and no friends
with these pieces, but he prided himself on his integrity. He
never wrote entirely admiring reviews: 'It's the essence of a
book never to be perfect,' he said, 'so its writer must expect
to come in for a little criticism.' They always came in for
more than a little if they had offended him in the past. It
was a great way to get revenge for various slights, lost jobs,
bad reviews or even undeserved success. Nigel resented
the attention that each and every author he reviewed was
getting. It ought to have been *his* work out there getting
a full half page.

He always brought his reviews into offices personally and
sometimes got taken out to lunch. It was nice not to have
to buy food. He always ate heartily on these occasions. He
would have liked to have taken a doggy bag to restaurants
and collar extras he couldn't quite fit in, like garlic bread,
crusty granary rolls and After Eights. He longed to take
away enough for breakfast or make a quick sandwich of
the hors d'oeuvres for later. Regretfully, he had to let it

all pass; he knew such behaviour would have created a bad impression with editors and got him laughed at – the thing he most feared.

He had stopped bringing groceries home, so the extras would have been useful. He never brought in anything unless he had plans to eat it right away. Then it was usually delicatessen, a filled roll or some cheese or fruit, anything that could be gobbled up quickly. Sometimes he went to his mother's for dinner. She fed him well, but he was not comfortable there, as she nearly always had a younger man around. Some of them were even younger than he.

Gina and Nigel had had no guests for a year now. Even Anthony was staying away. He was busy 'bumming his way round Europe' in imitation of his father. Nigel sometimes felt he didn't deserve such imitative admiration. He didn't tell Anthony that his parents had paid for his travels. Anthony was doing things the hard way. He had a manual of casual jobs – things like grape-picking, which had got him through the summer. He had even saved a little. It was harder to work casually in the winter, though. The pay is usually appalling for those who don't speak much of any language but their own and want cash in hand with few questions asked. The last Nigel heard, Anthony was working on an archaeological site in northern Italy. It wasn't a paid job. He just got dormitory accommodation and as much food as he could eat. Knowing Anthony's appetite that was probably a very fair deal, Nigel thought. He had always resented the amount his son ate. It seemed superhuman at times. Anthony would probably move on sooner or later; his bosses, two Anglo-Italian academics, had already warned him about the carelessness of his work. Anthony was fine with a pick, apparently, but when it came to scraping away layers of earth with a trowel and saving small pieces of pottery, he simply did not have the patience. Nigel was fond enough of him in his way, but he didn't want him coming home too soon. The house felt packed to overflowing with Anthony and his friends. Gina was even nastier to him when their son was there.

Nigel saw little of Gina these days. She was out every evening, sometimes staying away all night and coming back in the afternoon only to tart herself up for the next evening away. He didn't ask where she went. He had ceased to give her any money. Why should he keep her? She wasn't a proper wife to him any more. She could make a small amount singing, or whatever. She could get by on that. That was her business. She didn't eat much anyway, and looked thin and anorexic, even through her baggy clothes. He had hardly ever seen her naked since the first days of their marriage, and she hadn't been anxious to show herself even then. From the glimpses he'd caught he believed she'd had slight curves − he wouldn't have fancied her otherwise. He hadn't seen her eat anything for a long time. The last meal they'd had together was perhaps on holiday, or was it Eleanor's cake? But then she was out such a lot. He couldn't tell what she put away at her private views. He remembered, from the one or two he'd gone to with her, that she was in the habit of pocketing things and crunching large handfuls of crisps. She owned the packet of tea bags in the kitchen. They were going down gradually, so presumably she made herself tea when he wasn't around. Like him she never left food in the kitchen. Apart from the mess of dirty clothes in the bathroom, their house hardly looked lived in any longer.

Nigel sometimes wondered if Gina was well to be as thin as that. Maybe he should tell her to see a doctor. But then, he reasoned that was her business too. Perhaps she had already been to one. She wouldn't tell him anyway. He said 'You don't look well,' to her once, meaning to be sympathetic, but she clouted him and said, 'It is living with an old man that makes me not well. You do not look so well either.' He left her alone after that. If she was well enough to be nasty, there couldn't be much wrong at all.

Life grew greyer by the day, but Gina could always surprise him with new horrors. The latest was her glasses. She didn't need them badly. In fact, he believed she ought to have done without them for vanity's sake, as he did. No, instead she had got herself fitted with a big, bossy secretary's pair. When she was being important and rushing around she would push them up into her hair. At other times she would hold her scribblings at arm's length and let the glasses slide down her nose. The darned things never seemed to stay where they were meant to.

Gina had ditched her performing side. 'Too old,' Nigel had chuckled. But now, much worse than that, she was taking up writing. Her English was accurate enough, but there were slight awkwardnesses. He offered, in one of his kinder moods, to smooth these out for her. He would have liked her to be indebted to him for something. He could have stood the writing as long as she had looked up to him for guidance like one of his young workshop pupils. But her motives for writing seemed phoney – he believed it was just a form of competing with him and also imitation of Eleanor. She had seen how deep his admiration had gone.

Gina was writing stories to be like Eleanor and also poetry, in imitation of Nigel's youthful ambitions. She had even had some published in a horrible feminist magazine. Nigel figured they'd take any old crap by a woman. It was very embarrassing because she talked about the pain and degradation of sex and what a trap her marriage was. He couldn't remember ever being given much chance to degrade her. She hadn't complained about pain after that first night when she insisted on moving in and living with him permanently. He was the one who got degraded, there was no doubt about that. He was the one who'd been thumped, after all. He was far too much of a gentleman to degrade any woman. There were times, though, when he rather hoped a working-class bloke would take a shine to his wife and beat the hell out of her. He would have enjoyed being solicitous after – handing her the Vaseline, witch hazel and bandages with a pious lecture thrown in. Unfortunately, working-class blokes were far too sensible to take up with Gina. They had enough real problems.

Gina and Nigel had a big scene after the feminist publication came out. Nigel had got her measure enough by now to know that he would never be allowed to insist on anything, so he approached the subject carefully.

'You are a married woman,' he said in his best imitation of an authoritarian voice. 'If you must write — you don't need to by the way, I can earn enough to support my family — but if you really must, you should always write "Mrs Nigel Hughes" at the end of it and tell the editor you are married to me.'

'I do not want your stinking name,' Gina said. 'It has brought me nothing but trouble. It is common. It is common Welsh. There are hundreds and thousands of men and women called Hughes in your nasty cold country. I will use my own name. It is much more aristocratic. There were Buffons in the courts of the Bourbons and Catherine the Great. My grandmother told me so.'

'What as? Court jesters?' Nigel muttered sarcastically. Gina pretended not to hear.

'Oh yes, my family is much better than yours. I do not want my new friends to know I am connected to a boring man like you. From now on I will publish everything as Gina Buffon. I do not want to take your silly name any longer. If I had a wedding ring I would give it back. I do not want your emblems of slavery.'

Gina had once owned a wedding ring, but had chucked it at him in an early quarrel before disappearing for days. He had hidden it, thinking it would come in useful if he persuaded any girls to go away for the weekend with him. He had visions of booking in to the same hotel several weeks running and a knowing clerk saying, 'Ah, I see sir has a new Mrs Smith this weekend . . .' as his latest girl flashed her ring on the desk. He could feel the pride, but it was only a fantasy. When Nigel got brochures from country hotels, the prices — even the special offers — looked far from what he thought reasonable. No, if any girl wanted him she would have to provide the pad. She would if she really cared. That was what being a modern woman was all about. Nigel still hung on to the wedding ring. He told Gina he had sold it. Perhaps he would do so one day. He kept it, he told himself, to give back to her when she was kind and behaved like a proper wife.

It was more tolerable that his wife should write her horrible effusions as Gina Buffon (not many people knew his wife's name) but it was still more than he could bear. He tried to discourage her in every way. He played loud music if she was writing in the house. He made fun of any scraps of her work he came across. When these things didn't work, he got her fixed up with a particularly incompetent agent who had ruined some of his friends' contracts through laziness. If she still managed to get anything in the way of a book published he would persuade some friends to provide bad reviews. He was a man of influence in the literary world.

He felt caught between the frying pan and the fire with the literary women in his life. Eleanor's stories had made him jealous; his wife's effusions angered him. Now Eleanor had gone one step further. A colour supplement had published one of her stories in a series by new authors. He recognized himself in the main character. She had misunderstood the subtleties of their relationship and cast him as an ineffectual married man, always complaining of his wife, always on the chat-up, but never getting any further than that. He picked up the phone — his own for a change — and rang her in a state of anger. He pretended not to have read the piece. He didn't want to have to comment too much.

'Oh, Eleanor,' he faltered, 'it's Nigel. Something rather odd's happened. A friend has told me that you've satirized me thoroughly in a story and spilled some confidences about my wife. You wouldn't let out things I've told you in confidence, would you?'

'Oh yes I would,' Eleanor said. 'We're not friends any longer. You dropped me, remember, and in such a cruel way. Anyway,' she went on, softening slightly, 'that story's only fiction even if the James character is remarkably like you. Do you know, the editor of the *Observer* has had six married men ringing him this morning, threatening to sue for libel? Obviously they don't think it's you, if that's what you're worried about.'

Nigel assumed she was lying, but it made him feel better. He was sorry he had made a fool of himself by ringing.

'You understand the relationship's over?' he said primly.

'Oh yes,' she said. 'You've made yourself an enemy for life instead of a friend for life – very clever, that. I'd have done anything for you once upon a time. Now, I'm only interested in revenge. You told me all that stuff about your wife being unfaithful. You've given me a heck of a lot of ammunition.'

'I don't know what makes you think she's unfaithful,' Nigel said weakly. The conversation wasn't going the way he'd intended it to. He had hoped to make her apologize humbly and promise never to use him in a story again. 'I never actually told you she was unfaithful,' he said, truthfully enough. 'I only told you about her staying away a lot and men turning up looking for her and things like that. That doesn't really prove anything.'

'But what about the other address she keeps?' Eleanor asked.

'What do you mean?' Nigel asked. He was nonplussed.

'Don't you know?' Eleanor laughed scornfully. 'Look in the phone book. It's under Gina Hughes. I was looking for your number once. You wrote and told me to ring – presumably you were too mean to ring me – but you hadn't given me the number. Anyway, the Hugheses are all out of order in the book. British Telecom hasn't quite learnt the alphabet. Her name was there, in the wrong place. Don't pretend it's another Gina Hughes, because I'll tell you something more. Back in the bad old days when I was infatuated with you, I rang that number twice to find out. The first time I just heard a sort of brassy actor's voice with a bit of Northern in it, so I apologized and said it was a wrong number. I tried again a week later. I had worked out what I was going to say. I asked to speak to Gina Buffon. I told the man that I was a friend of hers before she married Nigel Hughes. He didn't deny any of that. He just said that she wasn't always at that address. Could I leave my number for her to ring me? I gave a phoney number and said my name was Claudia. It was the only Italian name I could think of in a hurry and I didn't have the nerve to put on the right accent to go with it.'

Nigel was disgusted but intrigued by the lengths Eleanor had gone to. 'You're barking up the wrong tree about the other address,' he bluffed. 'I did know about it, of course. It was just a bedsit she had early in our marriage when we parted for a while. We've been back together for so long I'd almost forgotten about it. We decided to keep it on and sub-let it as the rent was so low.' Nigel was not quite sure Eleanor believed him, but he knew he had presented a plausible explanation. That was the most he could do.

He said goodbye to Eleanor coolly, then looked in the phone book for the other number. He found it and rang it, giving exactly the same sort of excuse as Eleanor's. He left his own number, calling himself Alain – the name of her Malaysian-French 'business manager'.

The next day Gina rang. She had obviously not noticed that it was her own number.

'Alain?' she said.

'No, Nigel!' he replied with satisfaction. He felt a certain gratitude to Eleanor for giving him this idea.

'Oh, it is you, you lying pig,' Gina screamed. 'So, you have discovered my little secret!' She dropped the phone.

Nigel tried to confront her with her little secret that evening. But she just spat in his face and went out, slamming the door so hard that a picture of herself fell off the wall. He looked in the mirror and could see a gout of her smoker's phlegm on his cheek. She disgusted him more every day.

There was nothing more he could say in the way of argument, so he decided to plague her other address with mail. He searched through the free papers in the office when he took his article in, completing every possible coupon. He fitted her out with catalogues galore. He even sent £1.00 (refundable on order) for her to have a brochure of rubber rainwear and a free vibrator. That was all she was good for, he figured. Then there were free samples of pile ointment, Bob Martin's for constipated dogs (she was a bitch, he reasoned) and contraceptives. He phoned in her name and number in response to various job ads – masseuses, escorts and a lavatory cleaner. She would be inundated with calls. Then he sat down and typed a letter to every agony aunt he had ever heard of. He had worked out a basic form for this and photocopied it, leaving blanks to type in the appropriate names.

Dear

I have been married for nearly twenty-five years to a very nice kind Englishman. He is of a much better class than myself. I have been unfaithful throughout our marriage. I also hit him whenever I can and spit in his face. He is a famous writer, so I also tear up his manuscripts and books. I haven't had sex with him since the beginning of our marriage. I never cook for him and I am totally undomesticated. The only cleaning the house gets is when I force him to put the Hoover round on pain of a black eye. I don't have a proper job so I don't earn much money. Any money I earn I spend on myself or my lovers. When they visit I expect my husband to be polite to them.

My husband feels he ought to have someone else on the side. I would like to know two things:
(1) What you think of the way I have handled him?
(2) Is he entitled to a loving relationship with another woman?

Gina Buffon

That letter would really show her if it appeared in a magazine. It took him all day to find addresses and write the envelopes, as there are so many agony aunts in national newspapers, teenage and women's magazines. Some would of course reply personally (he had included postage). Those letters would be bound to point out to Gina how badly she'd treated him, telling her to reform and to save her marriage if they were religious, or else saying that she deserved it if he got someone else. That would put her in her place.

He went out that evening to his nearest post office. It was after hours, but he noted with pleasure that the letters would catch the 5.30 post the next morning.

In the middle of the night he had second thoughts and put on his clothes over his pyjamas. He wore silk ones – he liked to treat himself well. Part of the long top hung out beneath his short leather jacket and the material caught in the zip of his tight jeans. Still, no one would notice at 3 a.m. He went to the postbox. He had remembered it was nearly full with all the Christmas mail. He reached in carefully and pulled out a handful of letters. He took them to the nearest streetlamp to read the addresses. None of them were his. He left them on the road and went and tried again. As he fished, twisting his wrist back and forth, trying to get hold of more, a policeman came up and handed him the pile off the pavement. 'Haven't you forgotten these? Bit late posting our Christmas mail, aren't we sir?'

Nigel didn't like the sarcastic tone of modern policemen. They watched too many things like *Miami Vice* and had an exaggerated idea of their own importance. Gone were the days of the humble bobby. To put the man in his place, Nigel said that he was a writer who got his best ideas in the small hours. Unfortunately, PC Dickens happened to be a writer too. Although he was no relation to Charles, his surname had inspired him to pick up the pen. He insisted on sending some of his 'character sketches' about life in the Force to Nigel. He didn't need help placing them – the police have so many interesting in-house magazines with pictures of stolen *objets d'art* and jokes and stories in the back. All he wanted, he said, was a little constructive criticism.

Nigel went back home empty-handed and downhearted. He really hated literary wankers who sent him stuff to criticize. He'd never done that to anybody. What had he done in his last incarnation to deserve it? What sheer bad luck to meet a literary policeman when he was trying to do something nefarious but necessary. If any of those letters were published, and especially if they printed his initials at the end, someone – Eleanor for instance – might recognize Gina and himself. The story would spread. He decided to have flu.

CHAPTER
26

NIGEL'S FLU DIDN'T EARN HIM ANY SYMPATHY FROM GINA. SHE SEEMED rather happier than usual in fact. He spent the first day in bed, after going to the Chinese takeaway to make sure he didn't starve. He had an electric kettle, some lemons, a pot of honey and a bottle of whisky beside the bed, to make himself soothing drinks. The kettle and glass left rings on Gina's magazines. He was glad about that. It was rather nice being ill – he could get away with not clearing up his dishes.

At 1 a.m. Gina came in, switched the light on and woke him up. She bustled around, chucking her tights in the corner and putting on old ballet leggings and socks with holes in to keep warm. She went to the bathroom next and peed loudly. He thought she should have been a little quieter under the circumstances. 'Draw it mild,' he shouted. 'I'm ill!'

She came back dressed in her old sweaters, all her war paint still intact, and climbed in beside him. 'You're not ill, you're sick,' she said. It was a phrase of his she'd picked up. He'd used it about a lot of his friends behind their backs, particularly if they were homosexuals or had other sexual tastes he considered unusual. He comforted himself that his wife, being foreign, had just repeated the phrase parrot-fashion and didn't mean by it what he would have meant.

'You ought to wash all that stuff off, you'll damage your skin,' he told her, looking with distaste at her stale, badly applied make-up.

'You British wash too much,' Gina said. 'My father told me that a woman's body odour was the sexiest smell in the world.'

'Is that why your mother went round smelling like an

133

old goat?' Nigel quipped. He relished the usual kick in the shins. She didn't seem to be as strong as in her young days, and the socks stopped her catching him with her toenails.

The next day he went down unshaven to gather up his mail. He could see there were no cheques, alas. Most of it was just bumph, bills and Christmas cards, except for a bulky, strange-looking package which had been delivered by hand. He put that by for later. It might be a nice little present from a fan. Women occasionally sent him things, at least they used to – alcohol, aftershave or their knickers. There hadn't been so much of that though the last few years.

Later Nigel popped out to get some food, throwing a few clothes over his pyjamas. It was the weekend sell-by date in his local Holland and Barrett's, he'd remembered. There were usually some vegetarian pasties and things going cheap. He wasn't vegetarian, but he liked saving money when dining at home. Roast beef was for literary lunches. He collared a chilli-bean pie, a couple of samosas and an almond slice at 15p each. If Gina was pleasant to him she could share; if not, he would make them last for two meals. The old cow at the counter popped them in the microwave to warm them for him. He knew he could get away with asking her to do this – she had a bit of a weakness for him.

He rushed home with his hot food, mixed a lemon and honey with a large dash of whisky and proceeded to open his parcel. Gina was downstairs, pretending to write. The parcel was very well wrapped. He tore all the wrappings off like a child at Christmas and out gushed a welter of handwritten scripts. 'PC Motherfucking Plodding Dickens!' Nigel groaned. He dropped the lot into a shoe box and pushed them under the bed. He couldn't face it. It was enough to kill a writer who had flu. The top one was called 'A Modern Christmas Carol'. They probably did it at the policeman's ball. What on earth was he going to do? PC Dickens would probably find something to arrest him for if he wasn't nice about all this rubbish. The next time he was found drunk and disorderly he'd have had it. Or else he'd catch him shoplifting books, or catch Gina down the supermarket. Nigel was glad he'd sold the car years ago and not got another. Motoring offences are the traditional area for police revenge. They are very subjective, unlike shoplifting. Even if you're not parked on a yellow line, the police can imagine you're travelling at forty when you're just doing thirty and so on. Perhaps PC Dickens would arrest his wife for being drunk in charge of a bike with bald tyres? Now that might not be such a bad thing.

In the end Nigel decided to deal with the shoe boxful quickly. Fans hang over you if you don't do that. He said a few kind but ambiguous words about the pieces enclosed being 'eminently suitable for the audience they were aimed at' and left it at that. He would drop it off at the police station when he was well enough. It would save him postage. He would leave the packet open so that the desk sergeant saw they were not getting a parcel bomb.

By the third day Nigel realized it was boring staying in bed. He had panicked unnecessarily. Letters often took weeks to go into print, and the replies should teach Gina a thing or two. He went downstairs, finished his column, then shaved and bathed and went out to the office ripe for conquest. He could always have a relapse later if necessary.

There were only a few old women in the office. They seemed to be everywhere. Women lived too long these days. Part of him hankered after the poetic Victorian times when women died in childbirth at twenty leaving their partner free to get another young girl. Nigel had a quick look through the free papers, left his column on the editor's desk – he was still out for lunch – and shot off before any of the old women got any ideas. There were older women on the tube too. In fact they were everywhere. Perhaps he had run into a pensioners' outing. When he got home he was confronted by another older woman – his wife. He liked to rub in her few months extra from time to time. She was in a foul mood.

'Have you been to eleven Creffield Road?' he asked smugly.

'That is not your business!' she shouted and went upstairs to dress for the evening. He believed she must have received some of his mailings by now as she was in an even worse temper than usual. He quietly filled in a few more forms while she was changing. There were market-research questionnaires, trial subscriptions and a free assessment of your perfect man from a computer agency. He filled out all the forms making her older than she was and as uninteresting as possible. He wanted Gina to see herself as other people would see her. The perfect man the computer turned out would almost certainly be an extremely common old-age pensioner. She'd be lucky to get anyone in fact. Maybe the agency would write back telling her they had no one foul enough on their books. He hoped so. He had rigged the form that way. Perhaps he could drive Gina insane with a little more work. He fantasized about having her certified and getting a lot of sympathy. Then he realized that people would simply say, 'No wonder she went mad, living with that Nigel Hughes.' What he really needed to come out of this marriage smelling of roses was a lucky accident. Then Gina could become a beautiful memory. She was not sensitive enough to have died in childbirth like the women in nineteenth-century novels. Anything but a lucky accident might well make him look an idiot.

Lucky accidents never come to those who need them. Nigel was only a bit of a bastard and far too squeamish to stoop to murder. He and Gina went on living together and nagging each other quietly. He longed to ask her if she'd had anything nice in the post, but didn't quite dare. She was spending more and more time out — presumably she was at her other place. He would have liked her home more, because it made him feel in control. She was a poor companion — they had nothing in common — but he hated her being absent and was afraid that, one day, a friend of his would come to see him and ask where she was. Or perhaps somebody would phone, desperate to get in touch with her.

He imagined deaths in her family — some emergency. He would look such a fool if he had to tell someone on the end of the line that he didn't know where she was and had no idea when she was coming back.

Most of Nigel's worries proved groundless. There were no visitors to the house. His friends had stopped coming and the workshops he took these days were in colleges far afield. All the phone calls they received were for him, and Gina never had any mail. Perhaps she had given the other place as her address? He resented that and was determined that she should receive some mail at their address, under their married name. He filled in most of the coupons again and got a further selection of condoms, Bob Martin's and catalogues. As they arrived he would take them up to her in bed.

'Some post for you, Gina.'

To his disappointment Gina never opened any of her mail in front of him. She never brought back her correspondence from the other place, either. She simply got up, scrambled some old jeans on, pinched one of his shirts and went off on her bike. She packed her mail in the saddlebag. She rarely even stopped for tea. Sometimes he reproved her weakly about the shirts. She always spoiled them, getting indelible make-up stains on the collar and wearing them to a state of greyness for a week at least. He usually took his own washing to the laundry. He liked the service. Launderettes were for common people with common synthetic clothing. Most of his shirts were fine Sea-Island cotton. He hated having to hand in any that Gina had worn. When he did, the prim man who worked at the counter often inspected them and said, 'I doubt if this will come out, sir, but we'll do our best.' He believed the man must think he was gay and filthy, wearing shirts for a week and getting make-up on them.

He hated life even more with Gina away. He wrote one or two nostalgic short stories about the pangs of love, drawing on past memories and exaggerating them. These won him some critical praise. Women reviewers found them more sensitive than the stuff about his conquests.

The only time he saw Gina was in bed. He wondered why she bothered to come back at all. He hated her for making it impossible for him to bring women home. He fantasized about all the ones he could have had if only he'd been sure that a gnarled form in holey sweaters wouldn't join them at 1 a.m. He tried to tackle Gina about it, hinting that a young man like him needed sex from someone if he couldn't get it at home.

'I will lie back and think of the old circus days if you insist,' she said. 'But I will not enjoy it and I have an infection.'

He didn't like to ask what the infection was. Perhaps she was misusing English. She had often done that in the early days of their marriage, and he had found it quite charming. Perhaps she only meant she didn't want to give him her cold. That was rather considerate of her. Just in case it was anything venereal — though he didn't see what opportunities a woman of her age could have had for picking it up — he made sure that there was a larger gap than usual between them in bed. He showed concern for her and gave her an old, baggy sweater of his to put over the other garments. She had asked to borrow his pyjama bottoms but he drew the line at that.

Christmas was coming and Nigel hoped for a card from Eleanor. She had done him a beautiful hand-painted one the year before with 'Lots of love' on it. He thought hours of work must have gone into it. It had made Gina furious with jealousy. None of her admirers were as talented. 'Poor cow,' he'd said to her about Eleanor, 'she thinks she's going to get something out of me. She must be really desperate.' He had looked in the mirror after the card arrived. Yes, he was still as beautiful as ever. He didn't seem to age like other men. This year's card would relieve the monotony. He was beginning to think it would not have been such a bad thing if he had had an affair with Eleanor. His life seemed stuck in limbo with no sex and, worse still, no admiration.

Admiration was something he seemed to need most of all. He had no books on the agenda and most of the pupils in his workshops were men. Homosexual admiration was something he mistrusted. In any case, he didn't even get that now. Homosexuals seemed to have gone off him once he turned thirty.

CHAPTER
27

CHRISTMAS CAME AND WENT WITH NO CARD FROM ELEANOR. NIGEL realized then, for the first time, that his words had ruined their friendship for good. He regretted that. He was not one for burning his boats. He had always like to dangle women as long as he possibly could. He had reasoned that, like him, Eleanor would want to continue their friendship and sweep the quarrel under the carpet. She had seemed so smitten, he assumed there was nothing he could do that would really offend her.

Nigel was left with just one woman in his life to torment, which was only half the fun. His invention was flagging, too, torment-wise. His mailings were falling singularly flat with Gina. She was always in a terrible temper, it was true, but she never said anything directly about them. If only she had come in shouting 'What's this?' and chucked the lot at him, he would have felt something had been achieved. He was curious to know what had happened to the condoms, the Bob Martin's and the vibrator. He tried to visualize what he would have done with them. Being a man, he would have used the condoms and quietly dropped the other things through some charity shop's letter box. If it was an animal charity the Bob Martin's would come in useful. The vibrator, too, might well have some other application like soothing a dog's or an old lady's rheumatic shoulder. He figured that the women in those shops were too innocent to know what it was really used for. It was most infuriating not to know what Gina had done with all the free loot. Even if she hadn't sussed out who had ordered the stuff, she should have asked for his advice and help in disposing of it. He supposed that the man with the Northern actorish accent had given her all the advice she

140

needed. Perhaps he was selling it all off a stall or using the condoms on some young woman. Gina of course would be far too old to need things like that.

Nor had Nigel yet heard anything about the agony aunts' replies. He had not seen any of them in the papers, so some had probably replied personally. He'd have liked to have seen Gina reading one of their notes with a penitent expression. It was all extremely frustrating. He would have to think of some more immediate way of annoying Gina.

He was writing an article on 'A Man's View of Women's Magazines'. It was the first time he'd bothered to read through them and he found much useful material for his hobby of persecuting Gina. He found them enjoyable too and full of good advice on skin care. He took to cleansing, toning and moisturizing his face once he found that soap was bad for it. He was too conventional to use make-up but had no objection to skin-care products, eyelash or hair dye. He had to buy a lot of different numbers of magazines to do his research. It was to be a big article. Whenever possible he selected ones that contained pieces on the menopause and left them lying around where his wife could see them. He underlined passages about hot flushes and stress.

Gina tackled him eventually. 'I am too young for this,' she said and handed him an article in return on the male menopause. 'Men in their mid-forties often seek reassurance with younger girls', it said. Nigel was not amused. He countered by leaving other articles around on pre-menstrual tension. She couldn't have it both ways. There were better quotes he could underline here. There were incredible stories of battered, scratched husbands who sounded remarkably like himself. He began to be convinced that this might be Gina's problem until he monitored her nastiness. He kept a bedside diary giving her up to five stars a day for it. He wrote girls' phone numbers in the back of the book so that she would think the stars were for something else if she snooped around. By the end of two months, Nigel realized that his wife had permanent PMT. Only poison, not evening primrose oil, could cure that.

Nigel was getting bored with Gina's lack of reaction to anything he did. She hardly even spoke to him these days. He read another article which said: 'The average British couple watches television together for five hours every night and speaks about 150 words per person in conversation.' He wondered just how that had been assessed. Having a nosy reporter around might well make a difference. Still, it was another thing he could reproach Gina with that night in bed.

'We never watch television together and only say about fifty words a night, if that.'

'You are a boring shit,' she retorted, turning her back on him.

'You are a boring shit,' he mimicked, counting up the words on his fingers. 'Stop reading and put out the light. That was twelve — we are having a talkative day, aren't we?'

The article on women's magazines was spiked. A new female editor found it sexist. Nigel was paid for his work, but he hated not seeing his piece in print. He had worked so long on it and filled it full of malicious remarks at Gina's expense. He had been looking forward to showing it all to her. The bills were mounting up and Nigel seemed to be earning less and less. He knew he could always go to his mother for help, but pride stopped him. Gina never contributed a penny of anything she earned. She wouldn't tell him about her income, even when he was trying to fill in his tax forms. It had been an exceptionally lean year, all in all. He hadn't had a book out. His old royalties were down. The education cutbacks meant that most of his workshops and readings in universities had gone. With unsympathetic editors on the magazines he usually worked for, half of what he did was found fault with or refused. He sometimes wondered if Eleanor had put a curse on him. She looked a bit of a witch. He sometimes thought about ringing her and asking her to take it off, but common sense prevailed and he did nothing.

Nigel began to believe, if it wasn't Eleanor, it must be

his health that was at fault. He had been feeling depressed and lacking in energy. The novel he was supposed to be working on hardly progressed a few hundred words in a week. Something had to be done to get his energy level back to normal. He was not an old man. He started by reviewing his diet. Everything with additives had to go. On the one occasion that week that Gina brought home something, he complained about it. It was sausages – an old favourite. She seemed to have managed to collar a whole plate of them still on their sticks. In the old days he would have been amused and asked her how she'd done it. Had she pretended to wait on everybody at some private view, then walked out through the door? But now, sausages were a hidden enemy full of things like E-additives and monosodium glutamate. 'You're trying to kill me with cholesterol and all that E rubbish,' he said and stormed out. He went straight up to Oxford Street and bought a tracksuit. He had decided to take up jogging too. He was slim and attractive, certainly, but his body was not quite as tense and muscular as he felt it ought to be. A few weeks of this would set him up. All the young girls would be queuing then.

The first jog round the block got his heart racing and gave him an appetite. He was still supplementing his diet with various pills from his health shop. He added pumpkin-seed oil, ginseng, royal jelly and a herbal complex to boost his libido.

Nigel also took up aerobics at his local sports centre. He was the only man in the class, which meant he got a lot of attention. He believed it must be doing him good, and he could certainly feel the burn afterwards. By the third week the novelty had worn off, though. He had learnt as much as he could from the silly young woman teacher. All his classmates were either married with brats or disgustingly overweight. Some were both, in fact. He was horrified that women like that should think they were fit to be seen in leotards and striped leggings. When one of the fattest hailed him when he was out shopping he decided he must disassociate himself from that crowd. Jogging was more of a man's sport. He would stick to that.

In the weeks that followed, he found that the food supplements seemed to be making him put on weight, which was slightly worrying. The young health correspondent on a new glossy mag he was freelancing for said it could be one of three things. Perhaps his fat was turning to muscle. Perhaps the ginseng had altered the balance of his Yin and Yang, which can do absolutely anything to a man. Perhaps, on the other hand, he had a growth.

Nigel felt sure it must be a growth. He didn't know where it could be as he felt no pain except a slight stitch when he did aerobics. After three visits to his doctor, he was sent to hospital for various check-ups. He was so certain something was wrong with him that the doctor had to arrange an appointment to shut him up. Hospital was more comfortable than home, Nigel decided. You got fed regularly and women waited on you and asked you how you felt. One of the nurses seemed to fancy him. It wasn't every day she got such a good-looking patient. When his tests were all through, he decided to ask her out. He was wearing his new pyjamas and he lay back seductively. He had put a little bronze foundation on his face – a sample from one of the magazines. One look in the mirror he kept tucked away amongst his things by the bed told him that he was looking decidedly well. Perhaps he would take the nurse out on his way home from hospital. It would save him the fare. He was a little surprised when she said no and even more so when she told him that he was wasting the doctor's time – there were sick people waiting for these beds. 'Must be frustrated lust,' he quipped to the man in the next bed. 'Bloody nurses, think they're God's gift with their sexy stockings and belts.'

When he got home he started up his exercise routine again. He would stand in front of the bathroom mirror in his boxer shorts and expand his chest a few times, breathing deeply. Then he would touch his toes twenty times. Sometimes Gina sat on the lavatory watching him and making a bad smell or laughing. It was very off-putting. He didn't do any lying-down exercises because the floor was too filthy. 'If I get unhealthy because I can't do any sit-ups,' he told Gina, 'it's all your fault. You really ought to give the place a going-over with the Hoover once in a while.'

As soon as he was out of the bathroom he put on his track-suit and hit the road. He soon got to know the other joggers of the district. Most of them were so seedy he began to have doubts about the efficacy of his chosen sport. Half of them were old, bald men who nearly lost their elastic-waisted pants as they trotted round corners, puffing and blowing. They'd left it too late, poor sods. If only they'd started when they were young like himself, there might have been some hope for them. They were disgusting. They'd really let themselves go. They had probably never had his good looks, either. He came from a strikingly beautiful family, after all. When he got too puffed to run, Nigel would put one foot on someone's wall and retie his shoelace slowly. Then he'd bounce a little with his other leg out straight behind him to stretch his hamstrings and look like a proper athlete.

The jogging didn't really help his writing. When Nigel came back he usually spent some time checking his pulse rate. Often he lost count or forgot to multiply his fifteen seconds' worth by four to get the rate per minute. He was worried by the results, and thought he must be dying to have as feeble a pulse as that. He had believed after all the jogging that he would have the rate denoted as an athlete's on his chart. Sometimes he looked in the mirror and pulled his lower eyelids down to see if he had anaemia. He usually thought he did. Of course it might even be something more dramatic like leukaemia. He put this to Gina but she was not very sympathetic. She never had been when he was ill; that was one of the things he disliked about her – unwomanly, he called it.

Gina was annoyed by his jogging, though, that was one comfort. She had found the price tag off the tracksuit. It had been rather an expensive one as he had gone for a fleecy-lined designer number with flashes of blue, to match his eyes, on the shoulders and down the legs. 'You are a silly old man,' she told him, 'running along the road with everything jumping up and down. It is not attractive.'

'What about your lean old arse − I couldn't call it a bum in all conscience − grinding away on the saddle of your bike?' Nigel realized his verbal subtleties were probably lost on Gina. 'Arse' to him was purely functional − a container for an arsehole. 'Bum', on the other hand, sounded a more curved word. It was something that could be felt or pinched. 'You always leave your hair hanging down like a hippy too,' he continued. 'It's not the days of flower power now, whatever you may think. Next thing you'll be wearing a cow bell or painting daisies on yourself. Don't expect to be seen out with me if you do. And what about those shorts you wore last summer? You've got no meat on you. You shouldn't expose your lack of curves to the world. You could get arrested for cruelty.'

Nigel always felt he won hands down in a verbal fight. Being a man, he couldn't hit back when she started on him physically. Gina ran her bike over his foot viciously as she went out through the narrow hall. The handlebar caught him in the groin. It didn't hurt that much, but he pretended she'd got him in the balls, hoping for a little wifely penitence.

'I am so sorry,' she said, then went out shrieking with laughter.

CHAPTER
28

WHILE HE WAS STILL FEELING THE BRUISES FROM THE HANDLEBAR, Nigel sat down and wrote a story called 'The Illegal Divorce'. It was only about a thousand words long but of a high quality. It concerned a man who did not believe in real divorces. He was a very strong, patient, virile bloke who went on living with an awful woman because he had committed himself to a marriage. They had agreed to live as if they were divorced, but continue in the same house together. 'Sharing the same bed when the spark between you has gone has a particular pathos', he wrote. It was a subtle piece. He even put the woman's view to a certain extent: 'Miriam knew that their marriage was dead, but took comfort in the old rituals of going to bed together and getting up in the morning.' Even his feminist anti-fans couldn't quibble with that kind of sensitivity. Evidently the jogging was working. He was having new ideas at last.

He entered 'The Illegal Divorce' for a short story competition and won third prize. He would have been happy with that if only he hadn't been placed behind Eleanor. He avoided going to the prize-giving so that he wouldn't have to meet her.

Nigel always worked best when he drew on his own life. His articles on his childhood and schooldays had won praise from time to time from all but the most dour Communists, who resented his privileged background. There was no doubt that he could write well about high society, but the market for that sort of thing was dwindling. Most of today's moneyed people were jumped-up and took no interest in the old way of life. Nigel started to talk more about class in his new novel and less about twinkling nipples. He was beginning to realize he didn't have popular

147

appeal, so he thought he would try to mould his work into the sort of thing bought by a small book-buying elite. He would send notices of the book to his old school magazine and quietly pin up adverts for it in all the gentlemen's clubs in London. He didn't belong to any of them, but he knew the doormen wouldn't challenge a man with his distinguished appearance and well-tailored clothes.

As Nigel became class-conscious again, he resented Gina more and more. He had often told her that it was a social disadvantage having the sort of wife he couldn't take anywhere, but he dropped this line when she started appearing beside him at literary lunches and old school do's. Yet she might almost have passed, being foreign. A foreign accent is an unknown quantity; you have to be rather good at languages to tell whether it's common or not, and most of Nigel's acquaintances didn't speak any other language well. The main problem these days, however, was Gina's appearance, especially the clothes she wore. She now had a young designer friend who lent − Nigel sincerely hoped it wasn't sold − her a wide variety of sixties and seventies gear of the cheaper kind. She had smelly white plastic miniskirts with heavy steel chain belts that must have belonged to some fetishist, and acrylic ribbed halter-tops clinging to her almost concave tits. Often she wore platform heels and flared trousers. Worse still, after she had made a little money from the publication of a pamphlet containing her beastly poems about him, she commissioned a rubber dress from 'her designer'. She had it done cheap, promising to wear it in all the right places. It clung to all the wrong places. It was a sort of burnt orange colour with a large hole cut at the back so that the lean old arse Nigel hated so much could be shown to its full advantage. She got someone − he was glad it was not him − to apply orangey sun-tan make-up to her bare skin to match the dress. The first time she wore it, Nigel kept his coat on at a party so that he could hold the side out and cover the vision.

'Can't you have the decency to stand against a wall?' he hissed.

'That is not the point of Helmut's creation!' she said loudly, stamping on his foot and turning her bum out of range of his enveloping coat. She walked across the room slowly on her platform heels and joined the woman from her new feminist publishers. 'You see that over there?' she said loudly. 'It is my husband. The man in the poems.'

Nigel hoped his friends hadn't realized she meant him. He hoped too that she would alienate her feminist editor, Jess. A dress like that would certainly not appeal to the average feminist. Jess had short hair, no make-up and wore trousers. She would never wear rubber unless she became incontinent or was taking a course in scuba diving for women. Gina's rubber number was more suitable, he thought, for a pornographers' ball — if there is any such event in London's social calendar. On the way home in the taxi (Nigel was indulging them for once — he couldn't let Gina use her bike under the circumstances) he took delight in telling her she had a spot on her backside. 'I will squeeze it when we get home,' she said, unabashed. He vowed he'd put that line in his next book.

Nigel was unsure whether he hated the indecent rubber — which was at least up to date — or the flares most of all. He had offered to take them to the local dressmaker's to have them seamed in to a more fashionable line, but Gina wouldn't even let him do that. Nigel was very fashion-conscious. He believed if only his parents had given him more confidence and the right backing, he would have made a very good male model. He liked the fashion world and its reliance on youth. He liked the way female models were thrown on the scrapheap by their late twenties. Fashion knew a woman's place. Nigel liked looking at glossy magazines. There weren't really any proper ones for men, so he contented himself with *Vogue*, *Marie Claire* and *Harpers*. Luckily the local hairdresser's took them all so he didn't have to buy them. He preferred having his hair cut and blow-dried in a unisex salon, even if it was dearer. Sometimes he managed to abstract a page he particularly liked and take it home, He had a whole article on a young actress who had been asked to model some clothes. He pinned the photos inside his writing desk. (He had a school-type one – it seemed to suit him.) Every now and again, when he was writing, he would stop and lift the lid to gaze at Viola lounging in classic embroidered silks against the background of Hong Kong. She was remarkably like Eleanor, he thought, but better. She had that kind of gloss that only studio make-up and the last touches by a hairdresser can add. Better still, she was only twenty-two, not in her bloody thirties. After a week of feeling lovelorn and dreamy he decided to contact her. His balls ached at the thought of her. He was mystified by this phenomenon; it had never happened to him before, so he took it as a kind of omen. After the first exchange of letters, he would tell Viola about it to impress her of his need and, indeed, his right to her.

Nigel's first note had to be sent through the offices of *Vogue*. He knew that the office staff might open it and read it so he had to make it impersonal. He respected her talent as a model, he said, and would she tell him where she was performing? He would like to meet her. There was no reply for a week or two. He comforted himself by watching her on television. There was a brief interview on *Wogan*. She was all charm, all woman, he thought. Eventually, he got his reply – a theatre bill. She was playing the girl in *Equus*. He believed she must have sent him the bill personally, wanting to meet him as much as he wanted to meet her. He would treat himself to a seat in the front row.

Nigel went along on his own with a nice little pair of mother-of-pearl binoculars that had been in the family for generations. He wore his best suit, a clean silk shirt and shaved extra close. Actresses could see the faces in the first row. He tried to assume an amorous but handsome expression throughout the whole. It was hard, though. He had not realized that it would be the sort of modern play where people strip off and simulate the beginnings of a sexual encounter. Viola certainly had a nice body. He could see the texture of the skin – almost the down on it – through his powerful glasses. Still, he was shocked that she should have chosen to play such a part. She had talked of a sex scene when she was on *Wogan*, but he assumed it would be something more romantic – a magnolia bud of a tit peeping from beneath bed linen as she held out her arms to her lover and the lights went down at the end of the play. Getting her jeans off in two seconds flat in a stable was not what he had visualized for her. It had never occurred as a scenario in his fantasies. He had already dreamt about her often, but usually she was fully dressed and smiling enigmatically as she waited on him, bringing him food and wine.

He went round to the stage door afterwards and asked the man on duty to send up his name. Viola could not see him, the message came back. It was all a mistake of course. She must have remembered his name from the letter he had sent her. Probably she would know his books. She must have been gratified to hear from a famous person like himself. He realized that she already had fans, but the others were almost certainly complete wankers. As the doorman was unreasonable he would have to write another letter. He asked permission to leave it for her the following day. He could be more personal now that he didn't have to go through a nosy newspaper office. His first letter was just a simple out-of-season Valentine with his name and number on it to remind her. A few days passed and he heard nothing. Obviously he must write at greater length. That was what she expected of him. She must be trying to lure him to it, the naughty girl.

Poor Viola, she had just taken that indecent part for the money. He had to be charitable. Life was hard for actresses sometimes. His next letter offered her marriage to save her from the dreaful future of stripping off that she would be subjected to otherwise. He also told her about what she'd done to his balls. It was a twenty-page letter this time – in ink. Typing would have seemed too formal. It took him till nearly four o'clock in the morning. Gina lay beside him; she had nodded off and was snoring loudly. He despised her coarseness in being able to sleep with the light on.

By the second page he had decided not to tell Viola he was married already. When they had met and exchanged a few kisses, that would be time enough. He would go through the pain of divorce then if she really required it of him. That is, unless he was lucky enough to lose his wife in the near future. He had thought she was looking very old lately, and could pass for his mother when they were out together. If they both ran into Viola, he would introduce her as that, and if he waited awhile, fate might save him the trouble of a divorce, anyway. Then he could have Viola without resorting to sordid legal settlements. Gina had never contributed — why should she gain anything from him now? But, there again, actresses were known to be broad-minded. With a bit of luck, Viola might accept the existence of Gina and ignore her as he did. He would even be willing for Viola to move in and share their bed. They were all thin people — there'd almost have been room for a fourth person in the double his parents had bought him as a wedding present, so getting three people in it was certainly not an impossibility. He thought with disdain of the average British couple filling a bed with their protuberances.

If Viola were willing to come and live with him, they could have romantic evenings alone without Gina. He visualized simple dinners by the light of two candles with a single, long-stemmed rose in a glass between them. She would have rustled up a little casserole or *coq au vin* while he laid the table beautifully. Then they could have sex on a tiger skin by an open fire; actresses always owned things like tiger skins. All the sex would be over by the time Gina came back. At twelve or one, they would be sleeping idyllically, locked in a lovers' embrace. Gina could crawl in beside them or sleep on the sofa downstairs if she preferred.

Viola would have to give up her career, of course — otherwise she would be coming home the same time as Gina, which would not do at all. If she wanted, she could do a little daytime television work in one of the London studios. If she was tired when she came back, he might even cook for her – a few artfully scrambled eggs with a sprinkling of *fines herbes*. He didn't really approve of women earning a living, but the extra income would come in useful. She would have to be very selective, of course, and just do the odd, fully clothed, tasteful commercial for perfume or something. He put all this in his letter. He felt he was being particularly generous offering marriage to someone he had not yet met.

He mused on how different his life would have been if he had met Viola when he was twenty-two, or rather someone like her, for she would not even have been a twinkle in her parents' eyes at that stage. A cruel fate had separated them. He went to an Indian fortune-teller and asked for advice. The man talked a lot about karma and said that they had obviously been together in a previous incarnation, but now their birthdates were not synchronized. Perhaps they would come together in a future incarnation – not the next, probably, but perhaps the one after. Nigel gave up all belief in things occult after that and asked for his money back. The man told him in sarcastic tones that he could have his £9 back at any time if he brought in the young lady in the photograph. Indeed, he would even be glad to tell her fortune gratis if Nigel did that. He already had many clients from the world of showbusiness. The fortune-teller had obviously not appreciated his good looks, Nigel thought. The man wore thick glasses. Nigel muttered, 'You're as blind as a bat,' as he went out. He knew he was bound to pull any girl he set his mind on – he always had. Besides, the *Evening Standard*'s horoscope had said that tomorrow would be the start of a new phase of his romantic life. The envelope he found that morning looked like a reply from Viola. He knew it instinctively.

There was no letter inside, only a signed photograph. For a day, Nigel resented this, but then the photograph looked so beautiful and vulnerable that his heart melted. She wouldn't have sent it if she hadn't meant to encourage him. Perhaps she wasn't good at letter-writing. He could teach her. He left letter after letter at the stage door with no reply. Then he took to phoning. Her home number was not listed in the directory so it had to be the stage door. He had read the number off the old-fashioned dial phone as he handed his last letter in. He had a good head for numbers, and recited it all the way down St Martin's Lane and into Monmouth Street; then he went in a shop for a coffee and wrote it down on one of the paper napkins. He put this in the breast pocket of his leather jacket, next to his heart. He kept it there for weeks, later transferring the number to his Filofax. After a few days' dialling he knew it by heart.

Day after day, he was given the same old put-off by the stage doorman about Viola not being there. It was not a likely story when she was due on stage in half an hour. He caught her once on the way in. She looked pudgier and more ordinary without make-up, and he wasn't entirely sure she was the same girl. Perhaps it was just someone pretending to be Viola for security reaons. She was polite but cool. If it was Viola, she was obviously playing hard to get. When he finally got her on the phone, she only asked him how he was then said she had to rush, and put the receiver down before he had time to tell her. Obviously he had to put it in a letter.

He thought very carefully, this time, about what he was going to write, then decided to use the incident with the fortune-teller. He told her that he was going to continue writing to her, nothing deterred by her cold reply or rather lack of a reply. He had been to see a palmist and shown him her photo. He knew that their karma dictated that they would be together in various incarnations. If she did not believe him they could go together to the man. He practised just down the road from her theatre, above an occult shop in Monmouth Street. He had offered to tell her fortune for nothing if she went there with him. Nigel felt that was a good touch with which to end his loving letter. Actors were very superstitious, so surely she wouldn't be able to resist bait like that? He delivered the letter, together with a few flowers he'd nicked from a cemetery. They were large, impressive white chrysanthemums. He knew women couldn't resist flowers – Karen had once told him so. He had been almost tempted to buy some from her at a discount until he remembered her prices. Highgate Cemetery was more or less on his way to the theatre, and although it was almost all old graves without flowers, he had seen some being left regularly by some nutty Communist at the grave of Karl Marx. The woman would probably think it was kids who had stolen them. He left a token bloom behind, abstracting it carefully from the centre of the cellophane-wrapped bunch. He tucked his letter inside the pink bow.

At last there was a proper reply. He received it the next morning when he took his usual letter to the stage door. The flowers must have done something. It was rather hard to understand, though:

Dear Mr Hughes,

Thank you for the beautiful flowers. It was a kind thought. I must refuse the offer of a fortune, however. I have my own clairvoyant.

I was a bit puzzled by the card inside the flowers – 'To the greatest man who ever lived. Up the revolution.' Sorry, I don't get the joke.

I'd better ask you to stop writing. My boyfriend is getting rather jealous.

All the best,
Viola

'I'm the only boyfriend she's going to have,' Nigel said bitterly as he read her note.

CHAPTER
29

IN THE DAYS THAT FOLLOWED, NIGEL KICKED HIMSELF FOR NOT untying the bunch of flowers and looking to see if there was a card inside. A week later, while he was out jogging, he encountered the Commy old bat who had put the card in the flowers and made him look a fool to Viola. He deliberately ran against her, knocking her shoulder. He said 'Bitch!' audibly, then sprinted off leaving her in a state of stunned surprise. He had felt like beating her up, so it seemed a mild enough rebuke for the trouble she'd caused him.

He didn't know what to do to straighten things out with Viola. He felt he had made a fool of himself. With Eleanor it would have been easy. He could have told the whole thing against himself as a joke. He wrote to Viola again, saying that a spiteful florist he had once been kind to had put the card in the flowers. The card had really been intended for those regularly bought by a mad old lady to be laid beside the bust of Karl Marx in his local cemetery. It sounded quite plausible written down, and swapping cards was the sort of spiteful thing Karen might have done. 'Karl Marx must have had "To the most beautiful actress in the world and the one I love"', he lied.

Again there was no reply from Viola. Although he felt sure he would win her in the end, he was annoyed at her continuing coyness. It didn't come well from a girl who took her clothes off every night in front of an audience of five hundred, at least half of whom must be men. He continued posting his daily letters at the stage door, using his wife's bike to get there. He was a bit long in the legs for it so he sometimes knocked his knees painfully. He savoured the element of penance.

In the autumn there was to be a break in his usual routine. He had agreed to taking on a reading tour in Scotland. Someone from the publicity department of his publishers had set it up. The fees were ludicrously small, but it would be a good idea to get away from Viola. If she missed his letters for a few days, she would probably stop taking him for granted. With a bit of luck, she would be begging for it by the time he came back. Absence is supposed to make the heart grow fonder.

Nigel was really unwell at the last minute with a bad bout of flu, but decided not to cancel. He left one passionate goodbye note at the stage door on his way to the station. He promised to bring her back some Edinburgh rock — 'sweets to the sweet'. He arrived in Edinburgh that evening and was ferried by the organizer to his first reading at the university.

The reading was well attended by the students, but the occasion was short on material comforts. The air was thick with smoke and he was not offered dinner afterwards, merely driven back to the organizer's home many miles away. He had already christened his guide, who was from the local tourist board, Uncle Ebenezer. He felt sure the man had been paid some sort of allowance for putting him up, but it didn't look as if any of it was going to be spent on food. They stopped off for drinks in the country and it was about one o'clock in the morning before they were home. He could have done with something, fish and chips even, but the place was so goddamn countrified they probably didn't rise to things like that. He had to get up early to go on local radio, which meant another journey back into Edinburgh in the morning. From there it was on to more readings. The organizer seemed to eat nothing and offer nothing. Perhaps he popped out for a quick sandwich while Nigel read? By the evening of the second day, Nigel was fainting. He began to ask for orange juice when offered drinks, hoping for a little nourishment before he passed out. He eagerly grabbed any crisps that he found. In the middle of the night he rose and, after eating about half a jar of honey, felt a lot better. It was the only edible thing in the pantry. All his host's homemade pickles and stock showed an inch of blue mould. There were some joints in the depths of the freezer, but he didn't like to attack these. He also took a stick out of the packet of Edinburgh rock he had bought on the first day. He felt sure Viola wouldn't begrudge him that.

Mercifully, by the third day Nigel got some time on his own and was able to go out and buy a meal. He had had no key to the organizer's flat before so hadn't had this option. He spent the morning and afternoon looking round Edinburgh. Opting for a vast lunch in a pub, he ordered the dish of the day – haggis – then topped it off with a ploughman's lunch and the landlady's home-made black bun, much to the amazement of the proprietors. They asked him if he was English, then exchanged looks with each other. He also stocked up at a local health shop with various things he could nibble discreetly en route.

The fourth day it was on to Stirling and a literary society. He agreed to an impromptu reading in the evening only to find later that he would not be paid for it. It was an old folks' home. The old folks were not amused by his twinkling nipples and London escapades. One of them, with a yard of snot hanging from his nose, insisted on showing him some manuscripts he kept under his well-peed mattress. The old man said they were love songs he had written when young, but they seemed to be by Robert Burns as far as Nigel could remember. He admired them duly and was forced to join in with a chorus of auld lang syne downstairs. He felt like telling the old folk it was not New Year's Eve, but he doubted if they would believe him. He had only two more readings the next day, in Perth, before his release. He was driven by the local poet to a large school in the centre of the town. The man recited all the way and they were nearly late, with no time to stop for lunch. Nigel suddenly remembered Viola. All thoughts of her had vanished in the midst of his hunger pangs and coughing fits. He had taken a bottle of cough mixture with him but it hadn't helped much. Not one of the organizers had thought fit to provide a carafe of water.

'Could I possibly ring home?' he asked the headmaster. 'I'll pay for the call of course.' He was ushered into the headmaster's study and allowed a free call in privacy. He rang the stage door. There was a matinée, he'd remembered. He insisted peremptorily on speaking to Viola and she was called. He heard the stage doorman say, 'I'm sorry, Miss, but it's that old git who's horny about you. He just won't take no for an answer.' Viola was cold and distant and seemed determined to get rid of him. He put the phone down and had a violent coughing fit. He spat what looked like bloody phlegm into his paper hanky. 'TB,' he muttered, 'I must be dying of love.' Then he remembered the red lozenges he'd sucked all the way in the car.

At twenty-two, it seemed, Viola was too set in her ways for him. She looked like a beautiful young girl, but she had the hardness of an old woman. He wouldn't bother with her any more. She wasn't worth the effort, he decided. Perhaps he could pick up someone new today. He didn't often have the chance of meeting schoolgirls. They would be a better bet − you could see what you were getting. They weren't all covered in paint like actresses. Besides, he rather liked the uniforms.

Nigel read his sexier bits to the sixth form and they loved it. He felt sure the girls were creaming their pants for him. There was a blonde one with dark mascaraed lashes and a large bosom. She looked young but experienced, the sort that wouldn't waste too much of his time. He had decided to get away from his chaperons and ask her to his hotel for the night. He was being put up in a pub-turned-hotel in the centre of town. He thought he would phrase the invitation as 'a drink' − a knowing girl like that would take his meaning. He caught Moira when he was signing copies for the children. Several of them had bought his books, bringing out fivers like so much small change. Children nowadays were given too much pocket money. He had never let Anthony carry that much around.

Moira said she would ask her parents if she could have a drink with him. He didn't like the sound of that much, so he changed his mind and said he might not have time, anyway, after his other reading in a church hall. Moira went over to her friends and he saw them looking back at him and sniggering. The headmaster walked him across to his hotel and he was alone till evening.

He had brought his tracksuit and trainers with him to try to keep up his jogging. He had not been able to in Edinburgh, but now seemed the ideal time. A quick mile round the town, a shower and it would be time for the evening reading. He wouldn't eat in the hotel just yet in case the locals were feeling generous.

It was a fine bright day and he felt sure he had made the right decision. He pounded along the street and round two corners, losing his way. At the next turning he ran into Moira on her way home from school. He'd show the bitch. He lowered his tracksuit bottoms slightly as he slowed down. 'Hello,' he said as he stopped opposite her, dropping them below his prick. He liked to wear his fleecy tracksuit next to bare skin. He felt it would be a good idea to show her what she was missing by taking that 'I'll ask my parents' line. He was rather proud of his prick. It was long, thin, pale and sensitive – just like its owner. Moira screamed and ran away from him, dropping several books and a protractor. He gathered these up and sprinted after her. She screamed the more. He didn't mean any harm, he just wanted to give them back. As she turned into her house he threw her things into the doorway. He didn't know why she was screaming – he'd pulled his trousers up long ago. You can't run with your pants at half mast. He put his hand up her tunic – serve her right for having it so short – just as she got the door open and staggered screaming into her mother's arms. 'It's all a mistake,' he said, trying to follow, as the mother slammed the door.

He half expected that the police would be waiting for him when he got back to the pub. He ordered a pot of coffee to fortify himself and stepped into his shower. When he was dressed he sat on the bed wondering what to do. Maybe he could feign amnesia, or just cut the reading and head for home. It was unlikely that he'd get connections at this time, though. He thought about destroying his lovely tracksuit, but that would be a bit difficult when there was only a radiator in his room. Instead he opted for getting his penknife out and fraying the elastic in the waistband. If he could prove that it had too much give in it he would at least have a line of defence if he was summoned to court. He practised running on the spot. With a slight wiggle of the hips he could get his pants to descend below his buttocks after about twenty steps. He would go to his evening reading in his most respectable suit and brazen it out. Who would believe the word of a girl against his?

The reading came and went. By the end, although there weren't many in the audience, Nigel was feeling remarkably cocky. He'd got away with it completely. He had read some of the more discreet passages for the evening audience, having had a last-minute change of plan. Instead of the sexy bits he'd opted for poetic descriptions of London at night and the philosophic chapter from his last book about the beauties of a relationship between a young girl and an older man. The girl in the chapter was under-age, but the sex was so ambiguous and romantic that none but a prude could find it objectionable. Besides, age is in the eye of the beholder. He had pointed out as much to the audience.

At nine the headmaster, who had introduced him, escorted him back to his hotel and up to his room. Nigel assumed that he would lay on dinner. He tried to make small talk but got no replies. His bags were packed and waiting on the bed. The headmaster said, 'I think we'd better have a little talk. Young Moira McReady's parents have lodged a complaint.'

'They've got it all wrong. It was the elastic in my trousers. It could happen to any man.' Nigel pulled the offending tracksuit out of his case and demonstrated, pinging the elastic till it finally broke. 'These young girls, they're always seeing things. Wishful thinking, you know,' he said and nudged the headmaster.

'I know whom I believe,' Dr Kingsley said. 'I've told Moira to take tomorrow off to recover from her dreadful experience. The McReady family are all fine, upright townsfolk. Her father has been an elder of the kirk for the last twenty years. Moira's a fine girl too. We have great hopes for her.'

Nigel sat in depressed silence for a while. 'Well, get on with it – whatever you intend doing. You Scots are a miserable lot. I've had a hell of a time on this tour, you know. I'm not well either.'

'No, you're not at all well. I think that's the kindest interpretation we can put on it. I've phoned my friend at the hospital – a Dr Mackintosh. You can admit yourself as a patient tonight. If you won't do that, then the police will be called. We don't take kindly to perverts in Perth.'

Nigel decided to go to the hospital. The local magistrate might not believe in the frayed elastic, either, if the McReady family were pillars of the kirk. He thought he could talk his way out of this easily enough surrounded by educated people of a less prejudiced kind than Dr Kingsley. A mini-breakdown was less of a black mark than a criminal record if he should ever choose to emigrate. He only had one tiny conviction for shoplifting so far, and felt sure that wouldn't be held against him. He sometimes fantasized about emigrating, starting again in Hollywood where his looks and talent might be better appreciated. Besides, a part of him had always enjoyed hospitals.

CHAPTER

30

NIGEL FILLED OUT THE REQUISITE FORMS AT THE HOSPITAL DESK WITH Dr Kingsley standing over him. He was reminded of his own headmaster back at school. As he ticked 'married' the woman behind the desk asked if his wife knew he was coming in. 'It doesn't matter,' he said. 'We've been apart for a long time. If you like I'll give you the addresses of a few girlfriends. You can have my mother's address for next of kin.'

The Queen Victoria Memorial Hospital looked comfortable enough. It felt warmer than the pub. Nigel was given a sleeping pill and some cocoa before he went to bed. In spite of the pill he kept waking and hearing the old men around him coughing or mumbling in their sleep. The nurse on duty the next morning was pretty and obviously fancied him. Well, she would, wouldn't she? Even if he hadn't been such a good-looking chap, he was, by any standards, the only eligible man around. Everybody else there seemed to have Alzheimer's. Most were even older than the old folks of Stirling. He started to ask Flora, the nurse, for a relief massage. He'd seen a bit of that kind of thing going on in the last hospital he was in. Some of the nurses found it a nice little earner on top of their poor weekly pay. The man next to him there used to pretend to be in pain and put the nurse's hand on it. He tried the same with Flora but she only told him to save it for his interview with Dr Mackintosh that morning. 'We've heard all about you,' she said.

Dr Mackintosh was a red-faced Scot with mousy greying hair parted in the middle and tiny gold-rimmed glasses on the tip of his rather short nose. He studied Nigel's particulars and started to read them out slowly, looking

163

up to query various points and making notes on a pad in front of him. 'You say you're divorced, or is it separated? It might help us to get the full picture if we could talk to your wife. Perhaps you could give us her phone number. Did she remarry?'

'No, no, no! You've got it all wrong. We're still married but living apart in the same house, if you see what I mean. No, don't write down "no sexual relations".' Nigel couldn't actually see what the doctor was writing on the other side of his desk, but he could guess. Medical men were so unsubtle they usually jumped to conclusions like that. 'I'm a young man,' he went on. 'I have plenty of sexual relations with other people. My wife and I are just good friends. We live together, that's all. Anyway, I don't want to talk about that. It's all water under the bridge. I'm not a bloody American, you know — rushing to a shrink is not my idea of a hobby or a good day out. I'm a writer. We creative people live on a higher plane. We're all over-sexed like Picasso. That young girl yesterday led me on, whatever she says. It was an accident, anyway. I can show you the broken elastic in my tracksuit if you like. And I don't want to talk about yesterday either. I'm only here under duress because I didn't want to go to court over this nonsense. You can put down that I'm here under duress because your *friend*, Dr Kingsley, forced me to it. I bet he's not even a medical doctor either.'

'You're quite right. He got his PhD from St Andrews — a thesis on the poetry of T.S. Eliot with particular reference to *The Waste Land* as I recall.'

'Ruddy bank clerk — he would like Eliot!' Nigel muttered.

Dr Mackintosh went on, 'I don't take much pleasure in modern poetry myself. The only modern poems I enjoy are by Kipling. Now, you don't want to talk about your wife or about yesterday . . .'

'And I don't want to talk about my childhood,' Nigel cut in. 'I'm going to give you the score on that once and for all. I don't want to fuck my mother or murder my father.

He's dead already. You psychologists all have dirty minds. Who'd fancy their mother anyway? Mothers are too bloody old. Most wives are too bloody old, let alone mothers. I know mine is.'

'I see you gave your mother's name as next of kin,' the doctor went on unperturbed.

'Well, why not? The old girl should do her duty and send me a postcard if she can take the time off from her toy-boys. I've asked the nurse to ring my girlfriends too. It's nice to have a bit of attention when you're in hospital. The wife won't miss me. I'm an irrelevance as far as she's concerned. If she looks round one day for someone to borrow a fiver off she might, just might, notice I'm not there.'

Nigel didn't get any attention to speak of for the rest of that day. He just sat for a while in a sort of communal TV room with a few old loons. Some were knitting. Nigel had been offered wool and large blunt needles by an elderly nurse. The man on his left had been doing a scarf for a year, she said. He was very proud of it. It went all round the room and had ten different colours in it. One man was whimpering in the corner and two others were playing a bizarre version of dominoes, in which none of the numbers matched. Only they seemed to understand the rules; one of them turned round and stroked Nigel's knee. 'Piss off you old queer,' Nigel shouted. 'I can tell why you're in here.' The old loon looked puzzled and might have retaliated, but things were defused by a nurse bringing in the trolley of books that constituted the hospital library. The old man chose an Enid Blyton. Nigel leafed through a few large-print Agatha Christies but was put off by the noxious inexplicable stains on the pages.

The next morning brought a worried phone call from Nigel's mother, but nothing from either of his girlfriends. There was a local schoolteacher coming round to give art therapy; that at least should provide some light relief. She told him to call her Sheila, so she probably fancied him. She had wavy blond hair and was rather attractive apart from the beginnings of a moustache. He pondered on what kissing a woman with a moustache would be like. No, he didn't really fancy her, he just wanted to be praised and feel top of the class and get a little attention. He had been quite good at drawing when he was at school. He decided to do her a pastel sketch of himself having sex with Viola. That should grab her attention. He kept pulling his own and Viola's photographs from his pocket to check details. He always carried both photographs next to his heart. He got the facial resemblances easily enough, having a certain gift for hazy romantic portraiture. He had drawn his own face many times and Viola's once or twice before. He didn't like to make Viola completely naked – it seemed too prurient. Instead he did her in Eleanor's blue dress rucked up at the front to make entry possible. At the genital area he encountered graphical problems. It's hard to draw a prick in the act; they tend to be covered from sight in this position unless they are superhumanly long. In the end he settled for a rather Egyptian standing pose with both their faces front on and the bodies half turned away. He was naked except for a bow tie – a nice touch, that. Viola's right leg (stockinged) and a frizz of her pubic hair next to his would show the discerning viewer what was going on. He was rather proud of himself for being able to visualize and draw such a convoluted position. The smudginess of the pastels had helped him cover up early errors.

To his disappointment Sheila didn't praise him. She saved all her encouragement for a septuagenarian who had painstakingly completed a picture of a fishing boat with a peculiar figure like a tadpole standing next to it. 'Scottish Mafia, I expect,' Nigel said to her meaningfully. She looked puzzled. The sunniest pictures were pinned up on a board at the end of the ward. A few of the others were taken away, much to Nigel's annoyance. He saw now that they only wanted the darned things for analysis. He had really put both his feet in it. Next time he'd do them a bloody bunch of daffodils.

'A lot of blue in this picture of yours,' Mackintosh said the next day.

'I only put that dress on to cover up some bad drawing. Why doesn't this place provide models if they want us to get these things right?' Nigel replied defensively. He hedged at every new question. When the doctor opened a large book, he countered, 'I bet you're going to show me some bloody ink blots. My wife had a green one done of her body once. I've had it up to here with this naivety. Anybody who's not a shrink (or my wife) only sees an ink blot when they look at one. This is an absolute nuthouse. If I said I saw sex organs when I looked at your rotten ink blots that would really get you going, wouldn't it? I'm not going to please you by doing that. You can keep them and your art therapy. Yes, I know depressed people put blue in their pictures. But I'm not depressed. I counted up all the unbroken sticks of pastel and you cunning so-and-sos had put twice the number of pieces of blue there to catch us out. If I'd wanted to do red nipples there wasn't a decent whole stick of red left. That bloke who keeps pulling his double set of teeth out had pinched the lot. If I hadn't put that frock on the lady – she's my girlfriend by the way – I'd have had to give her blue nipples. I had to give myself grey ones as it was. You're just setting us all up to behave like nuts. I bet you go to the zoo with your kids and give the monkeys bananas, then complain when they jump around – the monkeys I mean. I suppose you're going to give me one of those American colour tests next. I know all about those. My son gave me one of them years ago. He was going out with a silly cow of an art student and she lent him the book. OK, I'll tell you what I got. I chose grey and black top of all, which meant I was a psychopath. I said to my son, "Well, I couldn't quite decide what to put first. Can I have another go?" I did and I chose black and grey that time round. That made me manic depressive. The bloke who made up those tests was the real loony if you ask me. Men and women have been choosing and wearing black for donkey's years. It must be about the most popular colour of all. Anyone interested in fashion and elegance would put black first. I certainly did.'

'You didn't tell me you had a son,' Mackintosh went on. 'Is he living with you?'

'Oh no, he buggered off to Australia on some scholarship. He can't stand his mother. Can't say I blame him. You wouldn't believe what I have to put up with. But then, you're too conventional to know anything about the sort of relationships that a literary man can have.'

'I'm going to suggest that you talk to one of my colleagues in future,' Dr Mackintosh said, keeping his temper. 'He is very interested in modern writing. Perhaps you might have something in common.'

Nigel was getting profoundly bored in hospital. He believed the nurses all fancied him, but none of them seemed willing to do anything about it. A couple of old ladies had raised their skirts and shown their NHS regulation knickers, but he wasn't tempted. The Cockney porter who had smuggled in a bottle of booze for him said that one of them liked to satisfy herself with the aid of bottle necks. He had hinted that it might be kind to pass the empty bottle of Scotch over when he'd drunk it. Nigel supposed it was just Cockney humour. Women wanted men not bottles.

'The doctors don't encourage sex between you lot,' Terry, the porter, went on. 'It's very unfair if you ask me. People have got to get their kicks somehow. I reckon it would stop a lot of trouble if they issued sex dolls in prisons and hospitals on the NHS.'

Nigel didn't like being lumped in with prisoners and mad women in this way. The man should have seen that he was a different sort of case and wouldn't be there for long. He thought about cutting him in future, but he was short of people to talk to. Instead he asked, 'How did a Cockney end up in this godforsaken spot?'

'Had to get as far as possible from the wife,' the man answered. Nigel could empathize with that.

There was remarkably little to do in the hospital if you didn't want to read Agatha Christie or knit half-mile scarves. Nigel decided to take up jogging again in the grounds and got Flora to lend him a sewing kit to mend his trousers. 'You will swear to the state of these before I mended them?' he said to her. 'I might have to go to court.'

The food was his only consolation. It was a bland, filling diet of the sort he liked and remembered from his prep school. He was sick of living on delicatessen from paper bags or literary lunches where *nouvelle cuisine* seemed to be the order of the day. He hated avocado, kiwis and limes, and everything in those circles seemed to have little snippets of these on top of it. Here things were much more to his taste. He liked the plain chops and boiled potatoes and greens; most of all he liked the rice puddings with a well of red jam in the centre and evaporated milk poured on to cool it all. The whole place was remarkably like school, only better. He had a little more respect here.

On the fourth day he received a long chatty letter from Eleanor. He had thought she'd rally round even though he hadn't been in touch for nearly a year. She was a sucker for his charm. She said she would visit; she was giving a talk in Newcastle and reckoned it wasn't that much further to come. She planned to stay for a couple of days in the Arts Club in Edinburgh, as she belonged to a London club that had a reciprocal arrangement. Nigel tarted himself up for the two days before her visit. He got the porter to buy him aftershave, but they didn't sell his musky expensive brand in Perth so he had to make do with a cheaper one from the tourist shop. It came in a tartan cardboard box and was labelled Highland Pea. Still, it didn't smell as bad as it sounded. It had a certain peaty resonance. Nigel donned his navy silk pyjamas and paisley dressing gown on the great day and prayed that nobody would be sick over him. He believed he looked ill bodily rather than mentally in his bed things. He didn't really want outsiders to know why he was there.

Nigel asked Eleanor into the TV lounge and they drank weak coffee from the machine. *Tom and Jerry* was on, but with the sound turned down. Nigel's mother had sent him some After Eights so he offered Eleanor one. She had brought some fruit. Remembering he didn't like grapes, she had lined up more exotic things like dates, kumquats and some out-of-season strawberries. He ate the strawberries quickly before anyone could ask him for one. He did not want Eleanor to talk to any of his fellow patients and suss out what sort of hospital he was in. The outside of the place looked innocent enough. 'I'm just in for a few tests,' he said. 'They don't think it's anything serious, but one has to be on the safe side.' He told her the whimpering man had cancer and had had his tongue amputated. It was a safe lie because the man never spoke. Eleanor would think he was in a cancer ward and be impressed by his bravery and pity him. Part of him longed to tell her the true tale, though, sending up the dour moralistic headmaster and the schoolgirl's screams at the sight of a perfectly natural part of his body. Eleanor had once joked that it was sexist that men were called criminals for flashing, while women were treated under the Mental Health Act. Come to think of it, he was almost being treated as a woman. Maybe Scottish law was different on this point, although, of course, the law as such had not been brought in. It had all been settled between gentlemen. It's hard to know where you stand when that happens. Eleanor would have been broad-minded enough to laugh at the whole tale. She called flashers 'failed comics'. On the other hand she might tell all afterwards when she got back to literary London. No, it was better to play for sympathy.

He sat back, as smug as a cat that has licked the cream, while Eleanor held his hand and looked concerned. She had obviously forgiven him now for all those cruel but necessary things he had said when he dropped her the year before. He was glad he had got the hospital to contact her. She could stay in Edinburgh for a few days longer, she said, until he was ready to go back. If it was only tests it shouldn't take too long. He felt proud when nurses passed and saw him with his girlfriend. They had to believe he was desirable now.

Nigel would have liked to discharge himself and travel back with Eleanor right away. He was only a voluntary patient, he supposed, and could leave at any time. Part of him yearned to start again. Perhaps Eleanor was strong enough to force Gina out of his life and house, and help him to a new beginning. 'I'll see what can be done,' he said. Visiting time was over and Eleanor left, promising to come back the following afternoon. He changed into his tracksuit when she had gone and went to talk to his doctors. Dr Mackintosh had left for the weekend, but Dr Lange, the literary one, would be free to see him in the morning.

CHAPTER 31

'I SAW YOUR GIRLFRIEND,' FLORA SAID WHEN THE EARLY-MORNING tea came round. 'Very pretty. Is she the one in the picture?' she went on, smirking slightly.

Nigel said that she was, assuming Flora had seen his pastel effort. Why disgrace Viola? Then he remembered the photograph that he left on his bedside table every night. 'My girlfriend's coming again today,' he said proudly. He was glad she thought Eleanor pretty. He had never been too sure as, technically, she was too old to come under the heading of pretty. Sometimes he believed that Eleanor was the love of his life. She was too old for him, it was true, but at least she was there. She noticed him, unlike his wife, and she had bothered to find out how he was. He wished he had a photograph of her. He couldn't keep pretending that Viola and Eleanor were the same person because Viola's photo was signed. Yet they *were* alike: Viola was a shade darker in skin and hair but the features were similar enough for there to be little difference between the two women in a picture. Perhaps he could obliterate the signature? But then, what would he do if Viola got time off from her play and came to see him, as she was surely bound to do sooner or later?

As soon as he was dressed, Nigel went to the main desk to ask if there was any post. It would be brought round if he waited, but he liked to have things as soon as they came. There were some Guernsey carnations from his mum and a card from Viola saying 'Get well soon'. He tried to read some deeper personal message into it. Why did she want him well? She must be after his body. He began to have slight doubts about going back with Eleanor.

He rather liked Dr Lange. He was a tall German who

spoke perfect English with only a slight trace of accent. He wondered how a German had ended up there. The nuthouse was turning out to be quite cosmopolitan with a Cockney and a German as well as the locals. The doctor was too young to have come over in the last war. He was only about Nigel's age, which meant that he'd have been a toddler then. He was the kind of man Nigel would have liked to have gone on the pick-up with. He had never in his life paired off to do this. He felt he would have been let down by his fellow journalists. They were all worse-looking and less refined than him and some were revoltingly overweight. His nights out looking for girls had always been insecure, lonely operations. With Dr Lange he would have had more confidence. Perhaps he would propose a night painting Perth red if there were any suitable local opportunities.

Dr Lange did at least pay him respect. He had read his first book, *Soho Nights*, and praised it knowledgeably. He also referred to Nigel's articles. Loath as Nigel was to cut into the flow of praise, he felt he ought to broach the subject of going home.

'Well,' Dr Lange said, 'you are of course free to leave. I wouldn't advise it, however. The brain of a writer is a particularly delicate instrument like the inner workings of a fine Swiss watch. While I was in Germany I took a special interest in the treatment of creative men and women who had lost direction and in some way broken down. I feel that you need a complete rest before you can resume normal life. In some cases, where the family is prepared to take special care of their loved ones, I would happily agree to a patient, or rather a writer, going home. But your case is different. If you were back in your own house and subject to the same old strains you might end up getting into the same sort of scrape again. What do you think?'

Nigel agreed that he might be tempted to behave in that way again. He was glad he had at last found someone who believed in his natural superiority. This doctor obviously had much more acumen than the locals. Nigel had begun to hate the Scots since being starved and caught flashing by them, but Dr Lange was different. Nigel could believe in him, and hinted as much. Perhaps resting there would not be such a bad thing for a week or two longer? He liked to think of the problems their unpaid bills might cause Gina.

'My colleague, Dr Mackintosh, has told me that you will not talk to him,' Lange went on. 'Now I have a suggestion to make. I believe that doctors and patients can have a friendly relationship. I would like you to think of me as a friend. If you feel like talking, talk. If not, fine. Now you are a very good writer. I would like to see some more of your work. In particular I would like to know about your own background rather than having to guess at this while reading about a set of fictional characters. I feel sure that you and your family are more interesting than some of these people you write about. After all, you are a creative genius and these characters are mere socialites. If you could see your way to writing the first chapters of an autobiography I would be honoured to read it and give you my thoughts on the subject. I think this might stop you feeling too bored while you're here. You must have found our library sadly deficient. In time, perhaps, you might like to borrow some of my books. I have most of the English classics. I am particularly fond of Dickens. Think about what I've said, anyway. If you feel like showing me a few pages in a day or two, I would be pleased, and I'm sure your other readers out there would be fascinated by a full autobiography. If you prefer to type, there's an old portable in the office that the staff never use. I'll tell them you can borrow it at any time. These hospitals all have computers now.'

Nigel was flattered and tempted. It was becoming harder to write at home with various thoughtless interruptions from Gina. A short spell of hard work in quiet surroundings would not be a bad thing. When he got back to London, he could perhaps pretend that he had been spending a few weeks in Hawthornden Castle on one of their writers' scholarships. He had given Gina a column to take in to his

174

paper while he was away. His only regular commitment was a fortnightly diary, so he wouldn't be missed for another week or two. With access to a typewriter he could even knock off another column about the lighter side of his literary tour, not mentioning any of the events at Perth.

Nigel was installed in the office with a blank sheet of paper in front of him when Eleanor arrived. Flora or somebody had told her where to find him. He had almost forgotten she was coming. She hadn't brought anything with her this time. He had hoped for some more kumquats, the man in the bed next to him having peeled them all.

'Are you feeling any better?' Eleanor said, bending over him and kissing him. There were no other chairs in the office so he couldn't ask her to sit down. 'Can we go somewhere and talk?'

Suddenly, Nigel felt annoyed by her manner and by the fact that she had brought him nothing. He liked to feel pampered not smothered. Eleanor was assuming too much in taking on the role of possessive girlfriend. 'Can't you leave me alone?' he said, brushing her hand off his shoulder. 'I'm trying to write. Can't you see that?'

'I'm sorry,' she said, her lip quivering.

Oh dear, he thought, she's going to cry and make me look a bastard in front of all the doctors and nurses. They might stop me having visitors if they think I reduce them to tears. What if Viola came and they turned her away?

'I suppose you're not coming back then?' Eleanor went on sadly.

'No,' Nigel said. 'I'm not coming back for a while. Look, I'd appreciate it if you'd do something for me.' He took her hand and looked at her winningly. She always fell for things like that; she was easy to manage. He knew he'd get his own way, although he was careful to use only his right hand. He had started wearing Gina's wedding ring on the other, wanting to show the nurses he was married. 'Be a darling,' he went on, 'don't mention I'm here to anybody. Maybe the tests will show it's all clear, maybe not. Anyway, I don't want their pity. I'd rather face up to

175

things alone. I'll get in touch when I'm back in London. I'll phone you then, or something.' He didn't really mean it, but his request sounded more gracious put that way. He imagined her waiting pathetically by the phone. She obviously wouldn't have anyone else at her time of life, in spite of all the men in her stories. 'You can send me the odd card if you like. You won't worry if I don't reply, will you? I would if I were my old healthy self. You know that, don't you?'

Eleanor told him she understood, kissed him and then left to start the long journey home. Nigel believed she would assume he had something incurable with a shade of film glamour to it — leukaemia, perhaps. He felt a weight lifted when she had gone — he had so nearly fallen into her trap. If he had allowed her to take him back to London, he might have been stuck for life with a woman in her thirties (and getting older by the day). She would have had a sort of power over him. Now, he was truly free for Viola. She was bound to come to see him sooner or later. He would take his ring off then. Maybe, if she was good, he would give it to her. In the meantime he was free to write. He started typing and found himself enjoying it for the first time for years. This would be his masterpiece. He read through his first paragraph — after years of novel-writing he found it easier to put it all in the third person.

'Once upon a time,' he had written. He was going to change that start later, but for now it was an easy lead in. 'Once upon a time, there was a boy called Nigel Charles Hughes. He came from a rich family and was very good-looking. He had a remarkable power over women. They all fancied him and thought he was the handsomest boy they had ever seen.... '

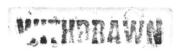